A HOBOSEXUAL YOU MAY KNOW

G.L. Williams

Copyright © 2022 G.L. Williams

No part of this book may be reproduced, distributed or used in any manner without prior written permission from the publisher or author. Exceptions given for quotations in book reviews, or as permitted by U. S. copyright law.

To request permission or contact the author:
BoarmanHolbrook@aol.com

Paperback ISBN: 979-8-9872489-1-1
Hardcopy ISBN: 979-8-9872489-2-8
Digital ISBN: 979-8-9872489-0-4
Audio ISBN: 979-8-9872489-3-5

Printed in The United States of America
First edition: November 2022

Published by Boarman-Holbrook Publications

The following is a work of fiction. Names, places, and events are the direct product of the authors imagination. Any resemblance to persons living or dead, real incidents or locations, is entirely coincidental.

TABLE OF CONTENTS

Introduction 1

The Story of Leon 5

CHAPTER ONE – Defining The Lifestyle 17

Sub One: First Things First 18

    "What is a Hobosexual?" 19

    "Is it illegal?" 21

    "Is it only Black men?" 23

    "Does it always involve sex?" 25

    "Could he have a job?" 27

    "The lottery question" 29

Sub Two: What Would You Do? 33

    The Story of The Writer 34

Sub Three: The Different Types 39

    "The Thief" 40

    "The Carrot Dangler" 43

    "The Popular Couch Jumper" 46

    "The Pretty Boy Trophy" 49

    "The Opportunist" 52

    "The Professional" 54

    The Story of Harold 56

CHAPTER TWO – How To Spot One 65

Sub One: Obvious Red Flags 66

    "He's homeless!" 67

    "Broke, but still dating!" 69

    "He uses a homebase!" 71

    "His first lie!" 73

Sub Two: What They Look Like? 75
    "All colors, shapes, and sizes!" 76
    "They're folks you know!" 78
    "He won't look needy!" 81
    "Too good to be true!" 83
Sub Three: He's Moving Quickly 86
    "Too quick to sleepover!" 87
    "Too quick to let you pay!" 89
    "Too quick to claim you!" 91
    "Too quick to claim your stuff, as his stuff!" 95
    The Story of Marcus 97
CHAPTER THREE – How They Do What They Do 111
Sub One: He's All Make-Believe 112
    "He lies for a living!" 113
    "Just a sprinkle of truth!" 116
    "It's everything you want to hear!" 118
    "He's a top-notch actor!" 121
Sub Two: They're Skilled At What They Do 123
    "He needs to be an asset!" 124
    "The Hobosexual okee-doke!" 127
    "He'll cloud your mind with orgasms!" 129
Sub Three: With Title Comes Power 131
    "Attachment co-signing" 132
    "Privileges of the babysitting stepdad" 135
    "Being your man insulates him" 137
    "Love means you're now responsible" 139
    The Story of Bobby 141
CHAPTER FOUR – Just How Dangerous Are They? 149
Sub One: Many Are Criminals 150
    "Some may rob you blind" 151

"Many are wanted men" 153
"The new online predator" 155
"What he knows makes him a threat" 158
Sub Two: Mentally And Physically Abusive 160
"Murder by a different name" 161
"They can become stalkers" 163
"From lover to witness" 166
"Dr Jekyll and Mr. Hyde" 168
Sub Three: Destruction In Their Wake 171
"Danger, the transmitted kind" 172
"Financial ruin" 175
"Scorched earth" 178
"Divide and conquer" 181
The Story of Tim 184
CHAPTER FIVE – How To Avoid Becoming A Victim 189
Sub One: If You Think It Can't Happen, It Likely Will 190
"The Scary biker" 191
"Thinking it could never happen to you" 192
"They're better than you" 195
"Beware of the convenient sleepover" 198
Sub Two: Just Don't Take His Word For It 201
"Check him out" 202
"Scrutinize everything" 205
"In the presence of his people" 207
"Remove your home from the equation" 209
Sub Three: Questions Needed To Be Asked & Answered 211
"Why are you crashing on someone's couch?" 212
"Why no job or income?" 214
"Have you ever been locked-up?" 216
"Why are you so comfortable dating while broke?" 219

The Story of Mr. Melton 221
CHAPTER SIX – What To Do If Victimized? 231
Sub One: It's Confirmed, You Have A Hobosexual 232
    "Don't show your hand right away" 233
    "Run him by the cops" 235
    "Get folks involved" 237
    "Time to get rid of him" 240
Sub Two: He's Gone, Now What? 245
    "Cut all ties" 246
    "Change-up" 248
    "The handy-dandy protective order" 250
    "Don't stay alone for a bit" 252
Sub Three: Your Show Must Go On 254
    "Don't beat yourself up" 255
    "Take responsibility for your mistakes" 257
    "Revenge hurts the both of you" 259
    "Share your story" 261
    The Story of Lou 263
EPILOGUE 277
ACKNOWLEDGEMENTS 281
ABOUT THE AUTHOR 283

INTRODUCTION
of a taboo topic!

I would like to take a bit of time to talk about a social predator that walks amongst us. He is not hidden, he doesn't stalk from the shadows, nor does he only prey on the weak and most vulnerable. Although he is a threat to us all, women tend to be his most favorite target. He attaches himself to you, then feeds just the way a leech does; or like a vampire, except this blood sucker just doesn't only come out after dusk. You can cross paths with him anyplace, anytime, anywhere. He'll cling on like a tick or flea, and feed until he's had his filling. And just like that tick and leech, unless you catch him in the act, you may not discover you've been bitten until after he's gone. But instead of leaving you with a small itchy rash, this predator most likely will leave you heartbroken and ashamed, and deep in debt. Meet the wrong one and you can find yourself mentally and physically abused, or even dead.

He's not a new phenomenon, this predator has been around since the beginning of time. I'm sure thousands of years ago there was a male neanderthal with only the rags on his back, standing outside the cave of a female neanderthal, trying to woo her to let him spend the night. I am sure there's some species of bird that instead of building a nest of its own, this bird simply searches for another bird that has a nest already built. And this lazy, no-good bird tries to sleep in the nest of the hardworking bird. I have no doubt in my mind if I researched it hard enough that I would find that this type of bird exists. If I'm not mistaken, I do believe I've watched a tv show on insects that spoke of a certain male bug that behaves this way. And as I'm sure you know, some things that a bug will do to another bug, you'll find a man that will do that same thing to another man, especially if that other man happens to be a woman.

Over the years there's been a ton of labels, a ton of names that have been associated with this particular type of man who preys on women this way: Scum of the earth, a bum, a con artist, a liar, and a thief. A low life son-of-a-bitch, a manipulator, and even a bullshitter. An asshole, a user, an abuser, and a rat. A cheat, a gold-digger, a loser, and a player. A modern day flim-flam-man, or a scoundrel. The last two being my personal favorites. They remind me of the villains in some of those classic films from the 1950's and 60's. While conducting my research, some victims used other descriptive words which I just don't feel comfortable repeating while my mom is still with us. Mom's still on that wash my mouth out with soap tip.

But for all the harm that this type of person has caused to a countless number of lives, to this day, he truly is a taboo topic. In preparation for this project, I spent a lot of time talking to people about him, my family, friends, and associates. Hell, I would discuss it with any stranger who would give me a few moments of their time. I found the subject alone made people uncomfortable, and I mean visibly uncomfortable. It was as if I was broaching a subject that was not supposed to be broached. You know, one of those topics that everyone has an opinion on, but no one wants to share that opinion? But like so many other issues that plague society, as long as the issue is a taboo one, the issue will continue to exist and prosper. You can't help people avoid leeches if we're reluctant to discuss leeches, and how leeches live. Same way with ticks and fleas, mosquitos, and the same way with this type of blood sucker.

When I asked my nearly seventy-year-old mother for her thoughts on this, she swore that she had never even heard of it. And my daughter Sydnie who was just nineteen at the time, well she claimed I was making it up. Karen, this schoolteacher I spoke to, couldn't believe any man would ever live that way. And regardless of how much I insisted that many men do, nothing that I said could convince her. My gym friend William said he personally knew a few dudes who preyed on women this way, but still he wasn't comfortable going into detail about it. While Stacey, an accountant that I had the pleasure of meeting one night while at a bar in Atlanta, told me her own father had lived that way for many years with her mom. And although no one in the family ever talked about it, everyone in the family knew he had.

Most people might not want to talk about it, but they damn sure need to be aware of his existence. It truly was, and still is a very sensitive subject. But together, we're about to change that. I'm going to take you on a stroll in the shoes of both the predator, as well as his prey. I'm going to familiarize you with how he does what he does, and who he likes to do it to. I'm going to introduce you to a Hobosexual that you may know.

The Story of Leon
"The Pretty Boy"

In the inner-city neighborhood where he was raised, Leon's gorgeous looks made him stand out like a single red rose, sprouting out of a weed garden. He belonged on the cover of some fashion magazine, at least that's what everyone always told him. The woman sharing this story with me described his face as perfect, and said he was one of the most attractive Black men she and many of her friends had ever seen in person. From her understanding, he did do some local fashion and runway modeling, she just didn't believe the modeling went any further outside the city in which they lived.

Although there was no doubt that all the guys wanted to be Leon, and all the ladies wanted to sleep with Leon; the truth of the matter was, Leon actually wanted to be one of the ladies, and sleep with all the guys. Unbeknownst to most outside of his immediate family and the local gay community, Leon was living on the downlow. You must understand, this was the 1980's, and during that era in the Black community, being a gay man could be a very tough road to openly walk down. So instead of skipping down the middle of that road for everyone to see, Leon chose to quietly tiptoe through the tulips alongside it, hoping no one would see him. But there were two things that everyone who really knew Leon was very much aware of: one, he never held a real job in his life. And two, Leon was a serious kleptomaniac, the man would steal and sell anything of value that wasn't tied down. He was what they called in the hood a "booster." If there was something you really wanted to get your hands on, but you didn't want to pay the in-store price, Leon was your guy to go to. He was a born thief.

Every inner-city neighborhood had a guy or gal that could get you anything that you needed, minus a store receipt of course. This unique skill contributed to Leon's many short stints behind bars. And it was behind bars where he honed his "using what he had, to get what he wanted" skills. It was also there that he discovered that gift wrapping his sexual prowess inside his extremely good looks, benefited him tremendously. Leon was a walking and talking debit card, all he had to do was find the right ATM to stick himself into.

During one particular time while locked up, this occasion for passing bad checks, Leon met Antwan. While Leon was just a petty thief, Antwan was a different animal all together. When they met, Antwan was in jail awaiting trial for drug distribution and attempted murder. It was alleged that Antwan shot a man in the ass for stealing drugs from a pusher who worked for him. Antwan was a street gangster, and anyone who crossed paths with him would tell you, he was not to be played with. He had a very violent reputation with the history to support that reputation. His appearance didn't help any, he sported a bald head with a few face tats, and a long scar from a knife fight stretched across the right side of his face. But as revered and feared as he was on the street, unlike Leon, Antwan didn't mind skipping proudly down that rainbow. Antwan lived as an openly gay man. And he fell head over heels for Leon, the day he laid eyes on him.

Although Leon hated being locked-up, for him serving time was actually a cake walk. His pretty-boy looks always put him in a position of never needing for anything, be it sex, drugs, food, or protection. Leon was a prize that many inmates who were looking for a cute boy-toy to snuggle with, would have turned down a pardon from the governor himself just to have Leon prancing around their cells in his jail-issued tighty-whities. And for protection and an open line to free commissary, Leon would gladly sport those tighty-whities for the biggest and baddest son-of-a-bitch he could find in his cellblock. And the biggest badass he chose to snuggle under during this particular vacation, was Antwan.

Antwan pulled some strings and had Leon moved into his cell and placed him under his protective wing. After that, no inmate dared look Leon's way. If one did, Antwan did not mind disciplining whoever did it, either with harsh words or with a shiv into the gut, it didn't make a difference to Antwan. Leon was his property, and everyone came to respect that, even the guards. And after just a few months of jailhouse marital bliss, it was obvious that Antwan had fallen in love with him. Although Leon did have feelings for him, those feelings was more for what Antwan was doing for him. As long as Antwan catered to his needs, Leon continued to play girlfriend to Antwan's boyfriend.

About a year and a half into his bit, Leon makes parole. Antwan promises Leon that if he stays loyal, he will continue to look out for Leon on the outside, the same way he was on the inside. Antwan was incarcerated, but he had a reach and influence that extended way beyond his cell bars. So as Leon kissed him goodbye, Antwan insisted Leon promise that he would remain his and his only until Antwan was also released. Leon gave him his word, despite being fully aware that while pledging loyalty to a man like Antwan had its advantages, it also certainly came with certain risk.

Remember, on the street, Leon didn't like having the gay tag attached to his name. And Antwan was a very well-known homosexual both in and out of the joint, so the last thing Leon wanted to get out was that he had become Antwan's snuggle bunny. Although he did have some feelings for

Antwan, he mainly agreed to stay loyal because he just didn't want to give up the benefits that came along with being the queen to Antwan's King. But the issue with being the other half of this particular king, was that Leon wouldn't be able to rip and run in the gay party scene the way he liked to do. Leon loved the nightlife, and everything that came along with it. He liked the risky sex, the boozing and drugs, basically everything that Antwan wouldn't accept his partner partaking in. Still, Leon promised Antwan he'd be a good boy, and headed back onto the streets.

This time in the free world, Leon found himself in a pickle. While locked-up, his mom, and only means of support, passed away after a stroke. You see, Leon never actually lived on his own, the only home he's ever known was the same one he grew up in. With nowhere to go, Leon ended up on the couch of the only person that would take him in, his older sister who not only didn't approve of his lifestyle, but who didn't trust him as far as she could throw him. Leon knew that living with her was going to be considered a short visit at best, and that short visit for him was going to be spent walking on eggshells. But just like he did with Antwan, Leon gave his word to his sister that he wouldn't get into any trouble. He did this, despite having neither the intention, nor the desire to keep his word to either one of them.

On the other hand, Antwan's word to Leon was as solid as it was when they shared a cell. Even on the outside, no one who knew he was Antwan's dared touch Leon. And if he found himself short on cash, Antwan would have one of his associates drop off a few bucks to him. Not much, just enough to keep Leon from going hungry, and keep a few bucks in his pocket. Most importantly, enough to keep Leon motivated to visit him at the jail a few times a month, but not enough to finance Leon getting himself into any trouble. But the truth of the matter was, unbeknownst to Leon at the time, the little money he was getting was just about all Antwan could scrape up. You see, by the time Leon met him, Antwan had already been locked-up and out of the drug game for a couple of years. Therefore, he didn't have the money, nor as much pull on the street as he once had. And to live the way Leon liked to live, that chump-change he was getting from his prison poppa just wasn't cutting it. And with his sister constantly reminding him that un-ass the sofa and get a job, there was only one way Leon knew how to supplement that small allowance he was getting from Antwan; Leon went back to doing what he knew best, boosting.

It doesn't take long for Leon to get his business back up and running. At the time, the popular item that was in demand on the street was prescription drugs. Stuff like Xanax, Percocet, Oxycodone, and Viagra. Leon had connections working in hospitals and pharmacies who would get him the stuff so he could sell it. He wasn't getting rich by any stretch of the imagination, just enough to keep him in the mall, and hitting the clubs just about every night. Anyway, he couldn't get really crazy with it because he didn't want Antwan to catch wind of what he was doing. And he definitely couldn't let his sister find out, she was just looking for a reason to toss him out onto the street. So, Leon continued buying his time as he waited for Antwan to get released. Then one day while meeting up with one of his hospital connections, Leon meets someone who would go on to change his life.

Angie was a registered nurse, divorced and living alone with no children. She's much older than Leon, and definitely not from the same side of the tracks as he's from. Angie was an educated woman, born and raised in suburban America, with about as much knowledge about the streets as Leon had about nursing. But of course, like any other woman who didn't know he was as gay as a pair of pink chaps, Angie wanted Leon the moment she laid eyes on him. And where she believed she may have just met the man of her dreams, Leon believed he could have just met another potential drug supplier within the hospital. But in an attempt not to expose what he was actually doing there, Leon played along with her flirting. After a brief conversation, the two exchange numbers and make plans to get together.

The next day, Angie picks Leon up from his sister's home and it was back to her place for dinner. She had a place out in the suburbs, about twenty-minutes outside the city, an area that Leon had never had a reason to venture into before. Leon was really impressed, Angie's home was really nice, the kind Leon had only dreamed of living in. Leon wasn't used to seeing Black people lived this way; single family homes with plenty of green grass at both ends of the house, and the stand-alone mailbox at the end of the driveway. He recalled seeing folks jogging up and down the block, which initially freaked him out because where he's from, seeing someone running usually meant there was trouble giving chase. But Leon played it cool and made his way inside. The moment he did, a smell hit him that he hadn't come across since his mother was alive. It was one of a home cooked meal, the one Angie had spent all day preparing for him. It turned out to be the best meal Leon had eaten since his mom. And later as he sipped his wine over dessert, it was at that moment that Leon decided that if he could help it, he was never gonna leave Angie's wonderful home.

Just like any man who spends just a little time alone with him, it wasn't long after they put down their forks, did Angie lead Leon back to her bedroom. He was gay, but Leon was willing to suit-up for the other team whenever he found it benefitted him. For some free meals like the one he just had, and a chance to sleep on a real bed instead of on his sister sofa, Leon was more than willing to switch teams for Angie. Sex was sex to him, and he prided himself in being a pro at it regardless of which side he was playing for. Needless to say, Angie was more than happy with his performance, Leon went out of his way to ensure that she was. He did things to her that she had never experienced. His goal was also to tire her out, so that she's too fatigued to take him home. His plan works like a charm. Leon spends the night, and it's the first evening since being paroled that he spends out of his sister's small apartment. The next morning, on her way to work, Angie drops Leon back off at his sister's. But before he could get out of her car, she practically begs him to come back over for dinner again after her shift at the hospital, and she wasn't taking no for an answer. Leon does his best to hide his joy as he accepts that second dinner invitation.

If he didn't know the first night, Leon definitely began to realize it the second night. Angie, like all the men he had ever given himself to, was already showing signs that she was willing to share everything that she had with him. And like all the others, he didn't have to do much more than keep her happy in bed and pretend to be into her as much as she obviously was already into him. He had been doing that with men most of his life, so that acting job wasn't gonna be too hard of a task. As he watched Angie in the kitchen cooking his favorite dish, spaghetti, Leon decided at that very moment that he was going to take full advantage of everything that she had to offer. And I do mean full advantage of everything. And it was that night that Leon kicked off his game plan

Leon starts out by convincing her that he recently discovered his sister is abusing drugs, and he's finding it difficult to remain roommates with her because of her addiction. Leon also goes on to paint a picture of his sister being a thief and a very unstable person who is constantly inviting unsavory people into their apartment. He tells Angie that if he doesn't find a new place to live soon, he's afraid of what he might get caught up in. And just like that, after only the second day of knowing Angie, Leon never returned to his sister's sofa.

But running the game on Angie wasn't as easy as he thought it was going to be. Not just because he was actually a gay man, but because he definitely had more feelings for Antwan than he ever could have for Angie. For Leon at that time, Angie was simply a way out of his current living situation, just until Antwan was able to get himself released. Even though Leon knew Antwan's chances of beating his charges and getting out were slim, Leon and Antwan still remained very hopeful that they would be together one day soon. Keeping the Angie train from derailing was not going to be easy. He was going to attempt to live with her, all the while keeping her from discovering what he really was, and about his boyfriend who was behind bars. He was going to have to pull this off, while also keeping Antwan believing he was still his queen, as he lived as Angie's king. This was going to be an extremely difficult juggling act even for an accomplished bullshitter like Leon to pull off.

As you would expect, it wasn't long after moving in with Angie, that Leon began to miss living his truth. Leon loved to party, more specifically he loved to party as a gay man. Afterwhile, he was often telling Angie that he was away at night visiting family, when it was one party after another, after another, after another. Amongst the gay community that knew him well, there was no secret about Leon being very free spirited when it came down to sex, or who he was having it with.

If living a secret life behind Angie's back wasn't bad enough, soon he was using Angie's money and car to facilitate that secret lifestyle. And if it wasn't with money that she freely was giving him, it was with money that he began stealing from her. After a couple of months, Leon gave up boosting and became totally dependent on Angie. And why not, she was totally comfortable taking care of him. Angie was feeding him, clothing him, putting money in his pocket; she was so blinded by how he was making her feel in bed, that she didn't see any of the obvious signs that he was using the hell out of her.

Leon grows so confident in his hold over Angie, that he tells her all about Antwan, of course leaving out the fact that they are lovers. Instead, he tells her that Antwan is his cousin. The only reason he tells her about Leon is because he needed Angie to be okay with Antwan calling her home collect from jail. Leon in turn tells Antwan that he moved out of his sister's apartment, and he's now living with his cousin Angie. Leon is confident that Antwan wouldn't really suspect anything was fishy because he's sure Antwan is convinced Leon is only into dudes. But still, he didn't want to take any chances. Angie doesn't suspect anything is fishy because she's convinced Leon is only into chicks. Leon was running some serious game on both of them. So much so, that not only does Angie allow the phone calls, but she also volunteers to drive Leon to visit Antwan a few times a month. That is until one of those visits turned out to be a visit that Leon would soon come to regret.

On this particular trip, the prison tells him that Antwan wouldn't be available for visits that day. Leon is told Antwan wasn't feeling well and was in the infirmary being checked out by medical staff. No matter how hard Leon tried to get more information, the jailers wouldn't budge on any. So, Leon returns home to await a phone call from Antwan. A couple of weeks goes by before Leon got Antwan's call, and Antwan tells him that he needed Leon to come back to the jail to see him as soon as he possibly could.

Leon returned to the jail the very next visitation day. And as soon as he laid eyes on Antwan, he knew something was wrong, very wrong. Antwan looked really sickly and weak; he had lost a ton of weight, his clothes now draping off of him as if they were two-sizes too big. Struggling to catch his breath, he told Leon that he wanted him to get a blood test right away because he was recently diagnosed with AIDS. But Leon isn't as shocked, or even as frightened as Antwan expected he would be. In fact, it appeared that Antwan was more concerned about Leon than Leon actually was concerned about himself. Without having any real reaction to the horrible news, Leon simply tells Antwan to take care of himself, then gets up, and leaves.

You see, Leon didn't have an emotional reaction because he knew something that up until that day, no one other than Leon's late mother had known. Leon wasn't devastated by Antwan's diagnosis, because Leon had known he was HIV positive for many years. And he kept that a secret just as he had tried to keep everything else about his sexuality a secret. So, like any other time someone that he was seeing ended up becoming sick, Leon simply turned his back on Antwan and moved on with his life, as if nothing happened.

As the months go by, Angie and Leon's relationship grows stronger and stronger. At least that's what Angie was thinking. When, in actuality, Leon's dependency on Angie was growing stronger and stronger. Angie starts introducing Leon as her man to her family, her friends and even her co-workers. The more she did that, the more power she gave Leon over her. The more she claimed him, the more of what's hers became his. And for Leon, the more empowered and in control he felt, the more outrageous and dangerous his secret lifestyle outside her home became. Now that he didn't feel obligated to Antwan anymore, Leon was really living recklessly. Unfortunately for Angie, she doesn't have a clue about any of it. Then all that changed one day while Leon was away, Angie takes a phone call from prison. And this time it's not Antwan calling collect.

It's the prison nurse, calling to inform Leon that his boyfriend Antwan had just passed away and had left all of his possessions to Leon. The nurse also informed Angie that because Antwan had died of AIDS, she was obligated to advise Leon that he should get himself tested as soon as possible. Angie is absolutely shocked and confused beyond words. But it was then and only then that many of the peculiar things about Leon that didn't make any sense to her before the phone call, only began to make sense. Things that just seemed to not add up, began adding up. Angie decides to keep the conversation with the nurse to herself, at least until she's gotten to visit her doctor and get some tests done herself, which she did that very same day.

When Angie hears back from her doctor, it's not the news that she wanted to receive. It instead was the worst she had ever received in her life. Angie was HIV positive. Armed with this horrific news, she immediately confronts Leon. Being the true conman that he was, he not only denied having HIV, but he also denied being gay. Leon tried to convince her that the prison was mistaken about his relationship with Antwan, insisting that Antwan was his cousin. When that didn't work, Leon attempted to turn the situation back on Angie's lap, telling her she was the blame for her sickness.

He accuses her of sleeping around with other men, and that's how she got infected. He even suggests that she had the disease before they met. But Angie is no longer under Leon's spell and insist that he get the hell out of her house at once.

I really wish I could conclude this story with a happy ending, but unfortunately, it didn't turn out that way for either Angie or Leon. This sad and unfortunate situation took place during the late eighties and early nineties, way before modern medicine had produced anything that allowed folks infected with HIV to live anything even resembling a normal life. In fact, most people who contracted HIV back then were reluctant to seek treatment due to the ridicule and often times unfair treatment that they received from those who discovered they had it. HIV at that time was almost certainly considered a death sentence. And once diagnosed with the AIDS virus, most folks wouldn't last another year.

Struggling to live with the disease, Angie eventually lost everything; her job, all her money to her extensive medical treatments, as well as her friends and loved ones who shamed her for having it. And when the virus began to really take a toll on her physically and mentally, Angie found herself living back home with her elderly grandmother, who was dealing with many health issues of her own. And after just a year of ridding herself of Leon, Angie died of pneumonia, which was caused by complications due to her battle with AIDS.

Leon was sent back to prison after Angie accused him of willfully and knowingly infecting her with HIV. While awaiting trial, because his case made the local news, more people came forward accusing him of doing the same thing to them. As a result, Leon's case went national, and he was one of the first to be prosecuted for sleeping with people and not revealing that he was a carrier of the deadly disease. Leon was eventually convicted on several counts and sentenced to fifteen years. And just a few years into his sentence, Leon himself succumbed to the virus in prison.

CHAPTER ONE
Defining The Lifestyle

Sub One:

First Things First

Top questions I always get:

"What is a Hobosexual?"

Depending on where you look and who you talk to, you'll find that there are various definitions going around to explain exactly what a Hobosexual is. Some acceptable definitions I have found are:

"A person who dates with the sole interest of having a place to stay."
"Someone homeless who enters a relationship just to find a home."
"A live-in relationship based on need and not love."
"Men who have sex with women just to have a place to live."
"A no-good, lazy, unemployed man who has a phony relationship with a woman just to stay off of the streets."
"A bum who tries to date a woman so that he can sleep in her bed."
"Any man having sex with a woman he really doesn't care for in order to keep a roof over his head."
"A person without a home who enters a relationship so that he has a place to stay."
"He's conman, who will attempt to trade lies, sex and companionship, for a spot on someone's couch or bed."

I could go on and on because there's a few more floating around, but you get the idea. For the most part, many of these definitions hit the mark right on the head. If you ask ten victims of ten different Hobosexuals, you are likely to get ten variations of what it's believed a Hobosexual is. Although each victim's story will be a bit different from one another, the testimonies will all be founded on the same element, which is the Hobosexual desperately needing a place to live. The methods and techniques he uses may differ, but the ultimate goal will always remain the same. And it's this common goal that will be the foundation for which we will stand on as we move forward in this project.

I did my best to incorporate as many of the definitions that I came across, as I took my own swing at defining the lifestyle as I interpreted it to be. So, for the sake of what I'm attempting to do here in these pages, my definition of a Hobosexual is:

"Someone who deceives and manipulates another person with the offer of sex and companionship, or with the promise of fulfilling a desire, for the sole purpose of maintaining a place to live."

You must keep in mind that my take on what a hobosexual is, is just that, my take on what a Hobosexual is. It's my definition; one that I personally believe most accurately describes the behavior. It's the definition that I find encompasses the totality of what it is, and the philosophy behind the lifestyle. In many cases throughout this project, you're going to find that you'll need to refer back to this definition to help you understand the behavior of both the perpetrators and their victims. It's important that you keep this definition in mind as we continue on.

"Is it illegal?"

No, Hobosexuality is not in itself an illegal act. Misleading another person for the purpose of having a place to live, is not against the law. It can be classified as wrong and immoral, but wrong and immoral doesn't necessarily get you placed in handcuffs. Hobosexuality is not something that you can be prosecuted for. So, unless during your time conning someone for a place to sleep you commit an actual crime, there's really no legal penalty that you can face. Most skilled Hobosexual's know how to use and abuse you in ways that do not put them in jeopardy of being arrested.

However, every day there are many crimes that are committed by people living as Hobosexuals. Crimes associated with this lifestyle choice can range from theft, embezzlement, check and credit card fraud, to burglary, breaking & entering, and up to stalking, assault, and murder. Although a Hobosexual committing crimes against you would represent the minority and not the majority, it's not a rare occurrence. A Hobosexual is more likely to steal your heart and time, than he is your money or jewelry. He's more likely to break your heart before breaking the law. It's why when many women find out that they have been victimized and reach out to their local law enforcement seeking some type of justice, they're usually disappointed to learn that there is really no justice to be found.

More often than not, it's going to be your bed or couch that he's after. Most Hobosexuals don't leave your home with anything other than what you've voluntarily offered or given them. Voluntarily being the key word in the way he operates. It's not actually against the law to mislead, to manipulate, or to deceive; these terms are not crimes, regardless of how much negativity is associated with them. Each action alone does not fall under the umbrella of criminal activity, it's only when these actions are connected to actual crimes are they liable under the law. Like misleading a friend in order to get them to loan you their car is not a crime. It's when you don't return that car when asked that makes it one. The "not returning it" can make it car theft. Or if you manipulate someone into allowing you to sleep on their couch and watch their tv is not a crime. But when you wake-up and you leave their house with their television, you're now a burglar. And that's surely one.

"Is it only Black men?"

Hobosexuality is most often associated with Black men, but the fact is anyone of any race, or any sexuality can be a Hobosexual. Although my book primarily depicts the experiences and accounts of Black perpetrators and Black victims, no group is immune from the existence of this type of social conman. From my research, I know for a fact that the gay community is plagued by them just as much as the straight community. The Hobosexual is an equal opportunity victimizer. But there is no argument that the term is mostly used in the Black community.

As a straight Black man, I'm naturally going to be more familiar with what occurs in the straight Black community. Although most of my life I have lived in truly diverse areas of the United States, the folks who I share a more intimate relationship have always been folks of color. So, the stories and point-of-views that I share with you will no doubt reflect this fact. But I did do my due diligence to learn as much as I could about the effect that Hobosexuality has on other communities, therefore I believe it's correct when I say that any person of any race can either be one or find themselves falling victim to one.

What goes on in one place, is usually going on in another place. Sex partners aside, you will usually find what happens within the gay community, happens in the straight community. In fact, the first time I even heard of the word Hobosexual being used was by a YouTuber who happened to be a gay Black man, speaking about gay Hobosexuals. And I instantly realized that his description described many straight men that I've known over my lifetime. But again, the term is usually associated with Black men only because it's in the Black community where the word I believe was birthed and is primarily used.

"Does it always involve sex?"

Definitely not. Sex is just his primary weapon of choice, the number one item in his arsenal. It's usually the key that he uses to unlock the door. The fact is, much of what he does to his victims is just as much mental as it is physical. Sex will always be the Hobosexual's go to method of manipulation when he first targets someone. It's his way of creating a bond with the person he's pursuing. It's the sharpest knife in his drawer, but not his only blade.

The obvious reason that sex is the number one strategy used by a Hobosexual is simply because it's free. It doesn't cost him one red cent to show you a good time in bed. So regardless of how down on his luck he is, as long as he can produce an erection, he has a way of keeping a roof over his head. He could be penniless, no car, barely a shirt on his back, but if he can convince a victim to invite him into her home, he will always have a way out of his predicament. It's a business that doesn't require any investment cash.

Under certain circumstances, sex isn't even a part of the Hobosexual's game plan at all. For example, a straight man who victimizes other straight men, is not using sex to run their game, but running game they still are. Instead of sex, a skilled Hobosexual will use whatever form of manipulation necessary to gain access to a targets home, and that form of manipulation is completely dependent on the target that they are victimizing. Most Hobosexuals are equally as good at whispering in your ear, as they are with having sex with you. He basically will try to satisfy whatever desire that he believes his victim needs satisfying. At the end of the day, it's not about sex, it about having a place to stay. A victim's wants will dictate how he will interact with them. So, if it's not sex, but something else that floats a victim's boat, he'll cater to that something else.

There are countless reports of straight male Hobosexuals victimizing straight male associates. Or straight females victimizing other straight females that they, of course, aren't in a sexual relationship with. As long as a person has a place that a Hobosexual can rest his or her head, that person is subject to being used and abused for those accommodations. He's focused on sleeping in your home, and he's gonna try to achieve that by any means necessary.

"Could he have a job?"

It's rare, but yes, some are indeed employed. Some have their own money and often times their own car, but it's definitely not the norm. In my opinion, having a job and money is one of the things that can make them so potentially hard to spot. Because if you cross paths with one that's holding down a job, you'll not be able to identify him as a conman because he won't appear needy or homeless. To the naked eye, the ones who have jobs and money will seem no different than any other guy trying to date you. Again, it's what can make him so hard to spot.

Some of them don't have a problem maintaining employment and spending their own money, they just have an issue spending their own money paying bills. Yes, the same bills that keep a roof over their heads, and the lights on underneath that roof. They would prefer that their victims cover all of that, they'd rather live on a victims dime. Any currency that they spend to maintain a place to stay would be in the form of sex and mental manipulation. Any money that he uses toward your home will only be to further cement his presence inside of it. Most of these conmen who are willing to keep a job will only do so in an effort to maintain his lifestyle outside of your home.

Because the Hobosexual is employed and has money, you can fall prey to him anywhere; your place of business, while out shopping, even the gym where you work out. You could meet him while on vacation, while eating in your favorite restaurant, or when attending your best friend's wedding. He can be found anywhere that you can be found. A Hobosexual who has his own money can use those funds to camouflage the fact that he needs a place to stay. So, chances are you won't know he's homeless until after he's moved in with you.

He'll use his employment and money as bait to lure a woman in for the kill. After initially moving into her home, he may volunteer to pay a bill or two just to trick you into believing he's a responsible person. It may not be until he's confident he has her properly hooked on his line that he'll start living his true self. And as soon as he does, he'll slowly transition from spending his own money, to only spending her money. Afterwhile, she's only getting lies and orgasms. And when he thinks that's no longer good enough for her, he'll move on to the next victim, and start his game all over again.

"The lottery question"

I once had a friend who hated his wife, I mean he couldn't stand the bitch. His words, not mine. At the time of penning this project, he had been with his wife for over twenty-five years. They both worked and split-up all the bills of the really lovely home in which they shared. Together, they were living the American dream; the big house with the white picket-fence, four lovely children, multiple cars, summer vacations, the full family package. But I promise you, whenever I would talk to him, he had no problem reminding me of how much he hated his wife. And knowing my friend the way I did, I knew he meant every word.

My friend didn't bring home as much as his wife, I believe he told me that her salary nearly doubled his own. He had no issue with admitting that he probably would not have been able to keep up that nice lifestyle if he were to take on everything without her. So, he put on a fake smile and did just enough in the relationship to keep her from asking for a divorce and leaving him to fend for himself. He could actually care less if she were to ever spend time with another man, just as long as she continued paying the majority of the bills while she did. In my opinion, my friend was living as a Hobosexual. A married Hobosexual. Not a Hobosexual in the traditional sense, but still a Hobosexual he was. He's misleading his wife into believing he really cares for her in order to keep her paying the bulk of the bills of the house that they shared. He was doing this, so that he could keep a roof over his head.

When I told my friend that I believed he was living as a Hobosexual, as I expected, he became terribly upset. He said he couldn't be one because not only was he married, but he was also at least paying some of the bills. But remember, many Hobosexuals will pay a bill or two. The fact is paying some bills doesn't exempt you from being a Hobosexual. The question I had my friend ask himself was would he continue to stay married if he could keep that same lifestyle he enjoyed without his wife's help? His answer was he'd instantly divorce her and leave if he could do it on his own. And it's there that he basically admits he's living as a Hobosexual, and he didn't even realize he was admitting to it.

The fact is, just because you don't think you are a Hobosexual, doesn't mean you aren't one. Just because you aren't willing to wear the jersey, doesn't mean you're not playing the game. Again, if you're living with someone that you really don't care for but only remain there in order to maintain a place to live, you could be a Hobosexual. You having love for the person that you're living with does not make you exempt from wearing the title. The fact of the matter is despite the love you feel, if you would move out the moment you could carry all the weight yourself, you are in my opinion, living as one. Sometimes it's not simply a question of do you love them, it may be a question of "why" you love them.

Most men living with women as boyfriends and husbands feel titles such as these obligates the women to take care of them when they are down. Regardless of how he really feels for her, if they're in a relationship, it's her job to provide a bed for him to sleep in. A man who thinks that way will never accept that he's living as a Hobosexual, even if he truly is doing so. It's the same way with a husband who doesn't like his wife but stays with her because he's out of work. He'll never consider himself a Hobosexual because the women he's living with wears the wife title.

A friend who lies to another friend in order to have a place to sleep is not going to accept someone calling him a Hobosexual, simply because the person he's living with is his friend. And why should he, when a friend supporting you when you are down is a responsibility that comes with being your friend. But it's what you're doing, not who you're doing it to that makes you a Hobosexual. It doesn't matter if it's someone who you just met, or someone you've known all your life, if you're misleading them in any way to persuade them to provide you with a place to stay, you're most likely living as a Hobosexual.

For anyone that is questioning whether they or someone that they know are currently living as a Hobosexual, there's one sure way you can figure it out. There's a question that I created that you could ask yourself, or one that you could pose to a friend that will help them find the answer that they're seeking. It's my "lottery question". But be warned, taking on this question, you could end up facing a reality that you're not really wanting to face. You may learn something about yourself that you may not be ready to learn. The question is simple:

"If you are currently living with someone who pays all the bills, or the bulk of the bills because for whatever reason you are unable to do so, if you were to win the lottery today for a million bucks, would you continue living with the person, or would you leave and get a place of your own?"

If your answer to this question is, "Yes, I'd leave," then there's a good chance you're currently living as a Hobosexual. If finances are the only thing that is keeping you where you currently live, there's a chance you're a Hobosexual. You're basically admitting that the only thing keeping you living with this person is your inability to live on your own. Regardless of how much you may care for them, the overwhelming reason you are remaining in the relationship is because they are financing your lifestyle. The question exposes a whole lot about how you're living, as well as a lot about your feelings toward your relationship. By saying that you'd leave if you were able to afford the getaway tells me that you're living somewhere that you really don't want to be, and if given the opportunity, you'd be out of there.

How you entered your living situation may not have been the traditional route that a true Hobosexual would enter a living situation, but the fact of the matter is you both could be remaining in your situations for all the same reasons. At a minimum, you both are lying by omission to the person you're living with. You both are avoiding telling the person you're with how you truly feel about them in order to keep them financing the roof that's over your head. You both most likely are having sex with someone who is under the impression that you would never leave them under any circumstances.

It's the quintessential "If you could do better, would you do better" debate. If lack of money is keeping you under that person's roof, you need to question if you're living as a Hobosexual or not. Are they really your better half, or are they really your care giver? This I know for sure and may be something you don't want to hear, but if you're broke and living with your wife or girlfriend, and a big check is the only thing standing between you and exiting out that front door, you are a Hobosexual my friend.

Sub Two:

What Would You Do?

Never say what you'd do in a situation, until you've faced that situation.

The Story of The Writer
"The Couch Jumping Opportunist"

Imagine being down on your luck, no job or money, no place to sleep. Everything that you own is stuffed into the trunk of your car. You're crashing on a friend's couch. And as much as your friend is trying to be there for you, your friend's patience is wearing thin, and he's looking for you to find another place to stay as soon as possible. But the problem is, you've run out of options. If your friend gives up on you, you literally may be living on the street.

One day you're sitting in Starbucks, typing away at that new screenplay you've spent the past few months trying to complete. You're also taking advantage of Starbucks' free Wi-Fi as you search online for a job, as well as a cheap motel that has a weekly rate you can afford, just in case your friend asks you to vacate his apartment. Your current predicament is a bad one, you feel the walls closing in on you and there's very little if anything that you can do about it. Then suddenly, an attractive woman sits down next to you and starts a conversation. It's obvious she's interested in you, it's obvious she's attracted to you, and it's obvious she's not aware that you don't have a pot to piss in or a window to throw it out of.

The two of you immediately hit it off, the friendly interaction is a great momentary distraction, and your spirits are lifted up a bit. She's a hairstylist, recently divorced, no children and living alone. You tell her that you're an aspiring writer working on your first novel, how you're relatively new in town, crashing with a friend until you find a place of your own. You tell her how the jobs back where you're from dried up, so you decided to come there in search of a fresh start. The conversation is going so well, you both don't notice the time flying by. Before you know it, the coffee spot is about to close and it's time for the two of you to part ways. But neither of you want the evening to end, so she invites you back to her place to continue getting to know each other over some red wine. You accept the offer and follow her home.

You're taken back by how nice and cozy her place is. She tells you to make yourself comfortable and you do, kicking off your shoes as you relax on her nice sofa. She hands you the remote to the big flat screen hanging on the wall. You begin scrolling, you've never seen so many channels, a person could never run out of stuff to watch. She orders your favorite pizza for dinner, and you're grateful for that because pizza is not a treat that currently fits into your limited budget.

She goes into the bedroom and changes into something more comfortable, which also happens to be extremely easy on your eyes. It's obviously not your first rodeo, you know exactly where her head is and where this situation is going. So, you gladly go along with the ride. As you wait for the arrival of the pizza, the two of you spend that thirty-five-minute delivery time getting to know each other more. You learn that she's forty-three, making her nearly twice as old as you. She doesn't date much because of the long hours that she spends working. In fact, she hasn't had a meaningful relationship since her divorce. A divorce that left her a bit broken because her husband didn't treat her very well. But now because she's getting older, she feels her window is quickly closing on her chances of meeting her Mister Right. It's at that moment you realize just how eager she is to toss her hat back into the dating pool.

The night continues on and turns into one of the best nights you've had in a long time. It's the same for her, she constantly tells you that it's been years since she's laughed so much. Although you're enjoying yourself, you can't help but think about the fact it's getting late, and you don't have a key to your friend's apartment where you're crashing. And because your friend is growing a bit tired of you freeloading on his couch, the last thing you want to do is have to wake him up so that he can open the door to let you in. But just as you begin to tell her that it's best that you be heading home, she makes her move and leads you into the bedroom. Again, it's not your first rodeo, so you gladly follow her lead. After an hour of making lovely mattress music, the two of you are now snuggled up under her nice soft sheets. She tells you that since it's so late, that you should just spend the night. You're happy that she offered because it was definitely too late for you to go knocking on your friend's door. So, you go out to your trunk, and grab some clothes to sleep in. She gives you a washcloth and towel so you can shower. After you clean up, you hit the sack and sleep like a baby. That is, after another round of sex.

The next morning when you wake, she's already up and has breakfast waiting. She talks about how much fun she had and invites you back over later that night to do it all over again. You both leave out together, her to work, and you back to your friend's apartment. You leave her place feeling great, not only is it the first time in a long while you had some adult fun, but it's also the first time in a while you actually slept in a bed instead of on a couch.

Just like the previous day, you start out at your friend's apartment, before heading back to Starbucks for some writing and some more free Wi-Fi. You stay there until your new lady friend calls to let you know she's home and that you can come back over. You get there, and the previous evening repeats itself. She orders food, you drink wine, watch a movie, and end the night having sex until you both fall asleep. This goes on every day for an entire week. Then on the morning of the eighth day, she suggests instead of you going back over to your friend's apartment while she's at work, you simply stay at her place until she gets off from work. And just like that, that initial one-night sleepover turned into a two-day, then a three and four-day sleepover, to you not returning to your friend's apartment for over a week. After a couple of weeks of this, you don't return to your friend's apartment at all.

This new woman is obviously really, really into you. And although you do like her, you're just not into her as much as she is into you. You instead are more into her cozy soft bed, the cable tv, her well stocked kitchen, and all the free meals she's cool with ordering or cooking whenever you get hungry. It's a hell of a better situation than back at your friend's spot. But because you know that she's really falling for you, you begin to feel guilty about not making her aware of how you actually feel about her. You don't say a word, not wanting to risk losing out on this wonderful situation. You continue to keep your mouth shut, as you go out of your way to keep a smile on her face. And it's at that exact moment, without intending to do so, you slipped into the world of Hobosexuality.

Unless you've been faced with the situation of being without any money and a place to sleep, none of us really know what we would do if we were to find ourselves in that predicament. It's easy to say or believe that we wouldn't stoop so low that we would mislead someone in order to keep a roof over our head. But quite frankly, you really don't know how far you'd stoop. Dire adversity can cause the best of us to act in very uncivil and dishonest ways. A person with food to eat should never say what they wouldn't do if faced with starvation, if they've never experienced starving. When the desire of self-preservation kicks in, there's no telling what you'd do to survive.

Most thieves weren't born thieves. Although there are people who get a thrill out of stealing, in actuality, most who steal do it because they feel they have no choice. Whether what they believe is true or not, it's what they believe. I tell people to never to claim what they would never do, instead, claim what they would want to believe they would never do. It's more of an honest way of trying to predict future behavior. Because one really doesn't know what one will do in the face of adversity, until faced with that adversity.

If you haven't already figured it out, the above story is loosely based off an experience I had with a woman name Kimberly nearly thirty-years ago. And for about six months, this beautiful, gentle, and intelligent person cared for me the way a woman felt she should care for a man who she loved and believed loved her back. And like the asshole I was, I took full advantage of that, up until the day I split. Kimberly was a great person, and I hope she found the true love that she was looking for, and deserved.

I once had a lifeguard tell me that when a person is drowning, they will drag their own parents under with them in an attempt to stay afloat. The person drowning is not using their best judgment when self-preservation and survival takes over. When you're unable to breath, breathing becomes the only thing on your mind, absolutely nothing else matters. And what you would never do one day, might be the first thing you do another day if you find yourself unable to breath.

Sub Three:

The Different Types

The six basic types of Hobosexuals you're likely to encounter are:

"The Thief"

One of the most destructive Hobosexuals you could ever allow to enter your home is the Hobosexual Thief. He can, and most likely will if allowed, rob you blind. From the loose change in the cup holder of your car, to using your debit or credit cards to steal thousands of dollars from your savings. If there's a way to clean you out, he'll do just that. He could even make off with your kid's piggy banks or video games. Sounds crazy, but it happens more times than you would like to know. If he thinks he can get a nickel for the urn that holds your late mothers' ashes, if you're dealing with a Hobosexual Thief, that urn is going to eventually come up missing.

Unfortunately, you may not realize that he is stealing from you until it's too late, until much of your stuff that's worth anything is gone for good. Or until he's gone for good. Most of the time he is going to continue to victimize you until he's no longer able to do so, or until the jig-is-up. Their goal is to come into your life and home, and milk you for all that they can milk you for before you catch wind of their con. Then he'll disappear like a thief in the night. Pun intended.

It's not unheard of for a Hobosexual Thief to be stealing from you in order to support some habit that you most likely won't know that they even have. And this scenario can make this type of Hobosexual a real problem. I've heard about many horrible situations of these men living with victims and the women didn't have a clue they were addicted to drugs, or even having a bad gambling problem. A woman not familiar with the symptoms of a person suffering from an addiction may not be able to recognize the signs. She may not even be able to conceive that someone she's falling for could even be an addict. And the more her mind is closed to the idea, the more she's actually opening herself up to the possibility of her being victimized by a man with a serious addiction.

There've been situations of Hobosexuals stealing money from women that they were living with in order to pay their overdue child support. And some of the women didn't even know that these men had children. Imagine, the new man that you moved in with you, is stealing from you and using your money to pay court ordered child support payments for children that you weren't even aware he had. Maybe it's not child support, but spousal support from a previous marriage. Either way, it's as foul as you can get.

Dealing with a Hobosexual is bad enough, but one that's a thief is a whole other can of worms all together. But most likely, one who is stealing money from you, is simply using that stolen cash to finance his lifestyle outside of your home. Without a job or any source of income, how else can he gas up his car if he has one? Where is he going to get the money to pay his car insurance, or finance any car repairs? How does he pay for his gym membership or cell phone payment if he doesn't get it from you?

Then there's that thief who is taking from you in order to woo his next potential victim. He's using your cash for dinner and lunch dates, flowers, and gifts, even trips and vacations. It's your money that he'll use to trick his next target into believing he doesn't need them for their money. He in fact is using their money he steals from you to butter-up the next piece of bread. Without even knowing it, you become an unwilling participant in the game he's running. By the time you realize you have brought a thief into your home, he's left you, and moved in with that next target that you helped financed him to obtain. And he's going to steal from her, just like he stole from you, and use her money to make a fool of the next target.

Frankly, most Hobosexual Thieves just can't help themselves. Stealing for them simply becomes habitual. They know no other way to survive other than living off of and stealing from their victims. Even if you are providing him with everything that they could want and need, this type of man is still going to rip you off every chance that he gets. It doesn't matter that you would freely give them the shirt off your back, they're gonna accept your shirt, and turn-around and steal a second and third shirt from out of your closet. If these particular conman had a choice between getting it for free or stealing it, many of them most likely will choose stealing it.

"The Carrot Dangler"

Mules are some of the most stubborn animals in existence. Hence the saying, "Stubborn as a mule." One of a mule's favorite things to eat are carrots. So, many years ago, farmers created a way to trick the mule to move in a direction in which the farmer needed the mule to move in. The trick was to dangle a carrot out in front of the mule, just out of its reach, and the mule would begin walking towards the carrot in an attempt to eat the carrot. The mule would be concentrating so much on trying to reach the carrot, that the farmer would be able to get it to go wherever the farmer needed it to go. He may not walk a mile in order to plow the fields, but he will walk a mile plowing the field as he's chasing after that carrot.

The Carrot Dangling Hobosexual is a man who promises their victim something that they know that their victim needs or desperately wants, in order to persuade the victim in to unknowingly providing the Hobosexual with what he needs or desperately wants. The Carrot Dangling Hobosexual dangles that promise out in front of his victim to keep her so focused on that promise that she is oblivious and blind to all the ways he's abusing and using her. He keeps his victims focused on one thing, giving him the ability to take advantage of her while he does another thing.

The promise you'll find most often used by a Hobosexual is the promise of a future long-term relationship such as marriage. Most women get themselves mixed-up with these men in the first place because of their romantic dreams of lifelong companionship, so it makes them easy targets for the Carrot Dangler. If his victim is concentrating on that relationship mirage that he floats out in front of her, the conman can get away with almost anything. I've even heard of a case where a woman being so convinced her Hobosexual was intending to marry her, that she went out and bought matching wedding bands, and spending thousands of dollars in planning the wedding. Only to discover weeks before the wedding what type of person her fiancé really was.

Then there's the carrot of future fortune, or the carrot of some sort of big payday. This carrot usually works with one of two types of victims; a woman who has her own but struggles a bit financially, or a woman who has dreams of living a rich and lavish lifestyle. Both types of victims can find themselves in a very vulnerable position when dealing with a skilled Carrot Dangler. Most folks want to live better than they currently do, regardless of how much they may have. The Carrot Dangling Hobosexual understands this fact very, very well.

He'll trick his victim into believing he's involved in some sort of business venture that's about to pay-off big. The business venture promise is always a good one to use, because it also allows the conman to justify why he has no money. He can claim his money is tied up in trying to make the venture come to fruition. He may claim there's an upcoming job that he's going to soon start that comes with a humongous salary. I've even heard of one dangling the promise of sharing an inheritance that he was gonna receive, despite the fact of course that there really wasn't any inheritance pending. If a Carrot Dangler suspects that his victim is beginning to doubt what he's saying, he will simply adjust his promise, or he'll create a new promise to hold out in front of his victim.

The goal of the Carrot Dangler is to keep up his charade just long enough for him to get everything he possibly can out of you. If you began to question why he hasn't married you yet, he will simply create a good excuse why he hasn't. Of course, whatever excuse he gives will be one capable of supporting his con. If after time you begin to wonder why his big payday hasn't arrived, a skilled Hobosexual will always have an explanation ready to feed you. The great new job he's waiting to start moved back his starting date. Or maybe the publishing company is asking for a few more edits to his new book before they release his big advance money. The fact is, if you have a question, a skilled Hobosexual will have a believable answer that you'll likely fall for. Especially if you're too busy captivated by that carrot that he's dangling out in front of you.

"The Popular Couch Jumper"

If he's on top of his game, this is the Hobosexual often times the most difficult to catch. It also happens to be the one that defies the belief that Hobosexuality is always about sex. Because most of the time the Couch Jumper does not use sex to manipulate his victims, he can simply use friendship or your admiration for him to victimize you. This particular Hobosexual can definitely be either male or female. He can be a dude sleeping on the couch of another dude, or it can be a chick crashing on the couch of another chick. He's not picky about who he targets, anyone that can provide him with a place to sleep is susceptible of getting taken.

When victimized by a Popular Couch Jumper, most males are victimized by male perpetrators, and females are usually victimized by other females. It's usually that new friend that knows you enjoy having him around that will use your fondness for him to influence you into letting him crash. That friend who you're probably already hanging out with, who already crashes at your place time to time, so it's really not a big deal to you when he asks if he can stay for a few weeks until he gets on his feet. He's that workout partner from the gym that you've become cool with who suddenly is in a bind and needs a place to stay for a few days. She's that new girl who you party with who always wants to sleep over after a late night of hanging out. They're that one homeboy or homegirl who always seem to be stretched out on a friends sofa.

In most cases, most single individuals really don't mind a friend sleeping over. That is until they notice it's happening a bit too often, or the friend starts to become an inconvenience. Like they're eating your food and never replenishing it. Or borrowing your car and returning the tank on empty. You start to see that they're not cleaning up behind themselves. Or the first time you spot that permanent butt indentation that's formed in your sofa cushion. The "enough is enough" day for me is usually when the friend asks if he could have his own key, so that he could come and go as he please. Or the day he began asking to not only sleep on my couch, but he's also asking to borrow some money.

Once this type of Hobosexual has in place a network of friends and sofas just like yours that's he's able to crash on, he'll always have a place to live, while at the same time having no place where he's required to pay rent. With that network in place, it gives him the ability to never overstay his welcome at one spot. And not overstaying his welcome on one couch gives him the ability to fly under the radar. Living this way, most of his friends won't even know that he is basically homeless. It's his ability to move back and forth amongst his friends that allows him to appear stable. Sometimes his network of friends won't even know each other, therefor when he leaves one couch to stay on another couch, the first friend may think that he simply has returned to his own home, the place where he actually lives.

He may keep small items at each location, a toothbrush and change of clothes, just enough for a few days stay, but not enough to raise eyebrows. Never enough of his stuff to make it look like he's actually living with you. Not enough that will cause you any discomfort or for you to complain that his stuff are getting in your way, but just enough stuff conveniently placed for him to use when sleeping over. For you, his personal items will simply appear to be items that he forgot to take with him, not items intentionally left behind.

He must be able to recognize when it's right to come stay with you, and when it is the right time to leave. He has to be able to identify when or if his presence may be becoming a nuisance to you. The key for him is to move on to another friend's couch before you want him off of yours. He knows that if it's his choice that he leaves and not yours, it's safe for him to assume he didn't overstay his welcome. Also, that way he can feel safe in assuming that you won't mind him staying over again when your couch comes up in the rotation. He wants to stay just long enough for you to enjoy having him over, but not long enough for you to grow tired or annoyed with his presence. There's a fine line he must walk, and great timing is crucial to not stepping over that fine line.

"The Pretty Boy Trophy"

Most Hobosexuals will likely be attractive. But the Pretty Boy, well, let's just say he's going to be extremely attractive. We're talking a prize possession, the trophy boyfriend. A man so good looking that his mere presence can hypnotize his victims into doing his bidding. He's what you want to see parading around your home all day, and trust me, he won't mind obliging you if it means he gets to live there for free. He's the man that has turned all your girlfriends faces green with envy.

Life for him has always been much easier than it has for others. He discovered early in life that he was special, that people would not only do for him, but most people wouldn't even require him to try to do for himself. It may have started back in school when as a youngster, teachers would tell him how cute and smart he was, even though he may have been the dumbest kid in class. Even the coaches would pick him to be on the team, even if he weren't good enough to be the water boy. All the chicks in the neighborhood wanted him, while all the boys wanted to be him. Again, he learned early that being eye candy made life really, really easy to navigate. The Pretty Boy knows that to most women that he meets, they're gonna most likely be attracted to him, and he's most likely gonna be able to get away with any and everything with them. If the Pretty Boy finds the right victim, he can live life like a king. Many women will do whatever or put up with whatever it takes to have that trophy boyfriend. Even if it means that they would have to take care of him as if he was a child.

I equate the Pretty Boy to the dumb blonde label. This is usually when a rich or powerful man gets him an extremely attractive, but not too smart woman to parade on his arm. Her job is simply to make the rich man look good, basically a trophy for the powerful man to show off. And like the dumb blonde, the Pretty Boy also doesn't have to be too bright, he doesn't even have to really be a good human being. He doesn't have to have a job, any money of his own, not even a promising future. All he must really be, is pretty. And of course, it's a bonus for the victim if he's good in bed.

Sometimes it may not be extremely good looks that make a Hobosexual a Pretty Boy. It could be another aspect of his person that can make him a prize that some women will eagerly want to possess. On occasion, he may be as ugly as a mule's ass and still be treated as a Pretty Boy. Instead of good looks, the victim may find something else very appealing about him. She may consider him to be a catch because of the beautiful car that he drives. To some, the more valuable the ride, the more valuable the man. Beautiful and expensive cars in most communities are a status symbol. To a lot of people, what you drive is much more important than what you look like. It's the reason why some Hobosexuals who cannot afford to keep a roof over their head, will beg, steal, and borrow money to keep a nice ride. Because they know that that nice car can open many doors for them, even if they know that they aren't worthy to enter through those doors.

As I'm sure you know, many women are attracted to the "bad boy" type. And for them, the more "gangsta", the more desirable he is. For some, a dude fresh out of prison with a criminal record as long as his arm is more attractive than a clean-cut male swimsuit model. He's usually the dude that the other dudes fear. He's the one with the reputation for being a bit unpredictable and wild. He may not have a penny to his name, but when he walks into a room, his confidence and demeanor captivates everyone.

Popularity can make a man extremely attractive. It's absolutely true that a person can become very desirable to one, simply because that person is found to be desirable to many. The fact that the Hobosexual is well known, or well renowned can also make him a hot commodity. He's the socialite who's the life of the party, but at the end of the night doesn't have a place to sleep. The artist, who despite everyone loving his work, he's completely broke because no one ever buys any of it. He's the singer in the choir that the entire church believes sings like an angel, so he always has a couch to sleep on, including yours. He's the down-on-his-luck ex-athlete that who although hasn't played a game in years, he's still the toast of the town. Hobosexuals such as these are not pretty in the normal since of the word, but their popularity makes them worthy of being a trophy on some woman's mantle.

"The Opportunist"

He's the one that could be living a normal, productive life one day, and then if the right woman with the right opportunity presents itself, he can quickly switch to living as a Hobosexual. He's the sometimes, or the parttime conman. Unlike the other types, he may even be very reluctant to even take on the lifestyle, unless he's really down on his luck and feels he has no other choice. But it is a skill that he has, so if he finds himself in a bad spot, he can easily resort to victimizing someone until he gets back on his feet. He's someone who actually may prefer to take care of himself, someone who really wants to live on the straight and narrow. Being a conman is not going to be his only talent. This person is someone you'll normally find gainfully employed. Under normal circumstances he's very self-sufficient, a very capable person.

Believe it or not, you may not only know many men like this, but you likely are related to one or two. For him, the lifestyle choice is predicated on the right situation meeting the right victim. This is the type of person who is definitely capable of maintaining a healthy and meaningful relationship where he takes on responsibilities of paying bills, and even leading a household. He can make someone a great husband, and he can be a great father to children. Again, if things are going well for him, you won't see a difference between him and any other man that you may get involved with. In this way he's like superman, who lives as Clark Kent until that tough situation presents itself and then he can no longer remain mild-mannered.

Many Opportunist Hobosexuals go on to live happy and productive lives, fully putting the lifestyle behind them, with no desire to ever pick it up again. He will completely place the things that he's done, and the women that he's done them to, in his rearview mirror. There are many women today who are currently married to men who have lived as Opportunist Hobosexuals. There are countless children who could never imagine that their dads were once an Opportunist Hobosexual. But Opportunist Hobosexuals they once were, and Opportunist Hobosexuals they will be again if placed in the right situation.

"The Professional"

He's all the other Hobosexuals rolled up into one, making him the deadliest social predator you can have the unfortunate luck of coming across. He's a rare one, he's the unicorn. He's the worse of the worse, he's going to be a problem for anyone to deal with. If you meet one, you have a serious problem on your hands. The Professional does it for a living, there's no other practical way to survive for him, nor is he looking for one. And he's an expert at what he does. He's going to be open to do whatever it takes to get the job done. He'll lie to you, just as quick as he will slap you upside your head if he feels it will keep you under his thumb. And if you don't freely give him money, he'll be happy with stealing it from you.

Paying bills is out of the question, regardless of how much money he may make or have. He's spending yours, and anyone else's money he can get his hands on. He's never going to sleep on a bed or sofa that belongs to him, it's going to be your bed or your sofa. The Professional will not only manipulate you so that he has a place to stay, but he's also looking to take you for all that you have. Any way that he can victimize you for his own personal gain, the Professional is gonna attempt to do that. And after he's cleaned you out, you'll never know you've been victimized until he's long gone. They are the best at getting away clean and unscathed. Being a Hobosexual is a job to him, and it's one that he takes very seriously.

The Professional is not, nor can he ever be considered your friend. You're just a mark for his con, you're simply prey, nothing more-nothing less. He's a conman through and through. And if you're in his life, you're being victimized somehow, someway. Anything a Professional says or does is part of a game he is running. Again, this Hobosexual is incapable of having an honest and genuine relationship with anyone. He will live off his own parents and siblings if given the chance.

The Professional normally targets victims that have a lot to lose, victims that he can gain a whole lot from conning. It usually takes much more than your warm bed to draw his attention. He's not looking to just survive, he's looking to prosper. He's gonna move on a woman who can allow him to maintain a certain lifestyle. It's the Professional who will marry, then divorce his victim for alimony. It's the Professional who will use sex to gain the trust of a woman of means, move in and manipulate her into investing in a business venture that he has. It's this highly skilled conman that will convince you to place property that you own into his name so that he can later sell it. He plays his game for high stakes, not just for a spot on your sofa.

It's victims of Professional Hobosexuals that you occasionally see testifying about how they were taken for all their money by a conman that they moved into their home; conmen who they later realized that he targeted them specifically because they were very well to do. And of course, when or if the authorities ever caught up with him, it's usually discovered that he's been victimizing unsuspecting women for many years. The majority of these women have been left penniless, and their lives devastated. He ingrains himself so deep into his victim's life and finances that when he moves on, the victim's lives are basically destroyed.

The Story of Harold
"Birth of a Professional"

    To better protect the prey, you must try to get to understand the predator. What experiences help create a mindset that looks at living off of other people, an attractive and practical way of living? And there's very little debating the fact that Harold was groomed from a very young age to be just that, a social predator. Harold was one of the most interesting Hobosexuals that I got the chance to get to know. He was what I call a Professional Hobosexual, and a very dangerous one at that. Dangerous because in every way that a Hobosexual could victimize you, Harold was proficient in each of those ways. Very smart and clever, and as manipulative as he was streetwise. For Harold, living as a Hobosexual wasn't just a skill that you reached for when you've fallen on hard times, for him it was a way of life, and the only one he ever knew. If you were in his life for any reason, he was most likely taking advantage of you, or trying to figure out how to. Like I said, Harold was a dangerous individual.

    I found Harold's beginnings much more intriguing and important to this project than any story of him living with a woman could ever be. And he had plenty of those stories for me to choose from. You see, I truly believe anyone could end up living as a Hobosexual; anyone from any aspect of society, any background, any race, or any religion. But after hearing about Harold's upbringing, I would have been surprised if he would have ended up being anything else but a social predator. Often times you really do become a product of your environment, you become what you see and what you hear. Most of the men that I spoke to talked about how when they were young, they all experienced seeing someone close to them using and abusing someone else. It had a dramatic and influencing effect on them. For Harold, seeing people used and abused was all that he saw as a child.

Harold never knew his dad, who skipped out on his mother before he was even born. The only thing he knew about him was that he was a horrible guy who when he was with Harold's mother, he treated her really badly, and fathered a few children with other women around town. Harold's life started out in the home of his grandmother. Also living there was his mother, his four sisters, a couple of aunts, and a cousin. He was the baby and the only male in the entire house. In my opinion, the sex of those that raise a boy isn't important, but instead the character of those raising him is. In Harold's case, it was the type of women who surrounded him as a child that caused his life to take some of the turns that it did. According to Harold, his household was full of users and abusers, crooks and thieves, liars, and drug addicts. And before Harold was out of diapers, these women were indoctrinating him into a lifestyle that would set his life on a course that would leave unmeasurable destruction in its wake.

As far back as Harold could remember, sex always played a major part in his life. Hearing his aunts and even his grandmother making love on the other side of a bedroom door is some of his oldest memories. If those in the house wasn't engaged in it, they didn't mind openly talking about it in front of young Harold. He was full of stories of him as a child playing with his toys as his aunts and their friends sat around discussing their sexual encounters. He wasn't sure if all the drinking and drug use didn't play a part in their ability to ignore the fact that he was in the room, as substance abuse ran rapid through most of his family members during those years. Harold claimed that he knew just as much about sex as most grown men by the time he was eight or nine years old. He recalled once in elementary school, a classmate reported him to the teacher because Harold was asking her if he could lick her until she came on his face. Something he no doubt picked up from someone in the house. He remembered how the only person who was angry about that incident at school was his mother, everyone else in the house laughed and joked about it. Harold's family just couldn't see that their nonchalant attitude toward him and sex was slowly creating a monster.

As a child, Harold didn't know how to interact with a female without it becoming sexual in some way. Any fun that he had with other children wasn't fun for him if it didn't include or end in someone touching someone else. Harold cringed as we talked and he thought about all the young girls in his neighborhood that he would go on to corrupt; young girls who should have been playing with dolls and skipping rope, instead of being taught how to perform the perfect doggy style position by young Harold. He couldn't even begin to remember all the virginities that he would go on to take.

The effect he had on the lives of the little boys growing up around him wasn't really any different. Harold himself admits he was a menace. If he wasn't teaching them how to run a train on a young girl, he was the kid bringing his friends in the house to watch the porn videos on the VHS tapes that his grandmother kept hidden underneath her mattress. Looking back on it, Harold believes he should have never been allowed to interact with anyone else's children.

When he turned nine, he, his mother and his siblings moved into a place of their own. His mom, who he loved dearly, worked as a live-in maid for some well-to-do family out in the suburbs. He recalled she would only come home a few times a month. When she did, she spent most of her time asleep in her bedroom with the door closed. Harold would never bother her, he understood she was only home to get some rest. After getting her needed rest, she would be home just long enough to make sure that the bills were paid, and that there was food in the kitchen. Harold described his mother as a good woman, who tried to keep him on the straight and narrow, it was just that she wasn't home enough to really pull that off. Taking from the playbook that her mother taught her from, Harold's mom was more concerned with providing for her children, then she was with teaching and guiding them. Harold was left to be raised, groomed, and molded into a man by his four sisters. His much older, attractive, and very street savvy sisters, who simply took over teaching him how to be a man, where his aunts and grandmother had left off.

For his sisters, the youngest being nine years older than Harold, not having their mom around and being in the inner-city environment in which they were in, gave them a bit more unsupervised freedom than they should have had. Even in their young teens, the girls were left on their own for the most part, and they took full advantage of it. Harold recalled how during the 80's, their house was considered the party house in the neighborhood. Although their mother didn't like people in her home, there was always people coming and going. Harold's sisters all being very attractive young ladies, seemed to always have guys hanging around. And Harold learned very early on that as long as there were guys around, his sisters always had money to spend.

As a kid, Harold would sometimes watch as his sisters would one by one, leave the house with men, only to get dropped back off sometime later with cash in their pockets. Usually just enough money to party and buy drugs with. But also, money that they happily spent on their little brother, buying Harold candy, or trips to McDonalds whenever he wanted. He recalled once when his mother was away and he needed thirty bucks for a school trip, one of his sisters simply made a phone call and a man dropped off the cash the morning of the trip. This type of thing happened a lot when he was a kid. A bill needed to be paid, or if there was no food in the fridge, his sisters had their own way of solving problems like these. Harold spent most of his youth studying his sisters closely. They were great teachers, and he was an eager and fast learner.

But because of the way his sisters openly talked about men around him, Harold felt as though his sisters really didn't like men, instead they only liked what men did for them. It was if that's all that they thought guys were good for. He never in his life saw one of them give a man any attention if that man wasn't somehow paying for that attention. He also recalled never seeing any sister having a relationship with just one man. They always dealt with multiple at the same time, with all of the men in some way taking care of them.

When I asked him why he thought his sisters were like that, why they seem to have very little respect for men, he told me he believed it was because of the hatred that they had for their father for abandoning them and allowing the family to struggle the way his family did. Also, unlike Harold, his sisters got to see his father abuse their mother. Harold believed it was because of their father being who and what he was, that his sisters came to really hate and then mistreat men. This sour seed toward their father was planted in the girls pretty early on because of how badly their mother spoke about her disdain for their father when the girls were very young. Harold also held a certain resentment toward his father because of the horrible things his mother and sisters used to say about him.

Just like Harold learned from watching his sisters, his sisters grew up learning from watching their older family members, like his aunts. Concepts like marriage and monogamous relationships was something that they only got to see on television. The only man Harold and his sisters ever had in their lives was their grandmother's boyfriend who they called Mr. Butch. And it turned out that the whole time he was in their lives, Mr. Butch was a married with a family of his own, who their grandmother was having an affair with. Whenever Mr. Butch would visit his grandmother, Harold and his sisters would watch as his grandmother and aunts spent most of their time finagling money off of him.

There were also always rumors that spread amongst the family about Mr. Butch secretly sleeping with Harold's aunts when they were just teenagers. Harold wasn't sure if the rumors were true, but knowing his family, he said it wouldn't surprise him if they were. When Mr. Butch died, Harold's grandmother, nor anyone in his family, was allowed to attend the funeral, even though Mr. Butch was like family to them. But Mr. Butch's real wife and kids didn't want any of Harold's family anywhere near the ceremony. It was the price Harold's family had to pay for being the "side" family.

Harold told me that as far as he knew, the women in his family only knew how to live one of two ways, either they were taking advantage of and living off of some man, or they were taking advantage of and living off of the government. I gathered that growing up seeing this really affected Harold in a number of ways: First, I believe it formed his belief that if a person claims to like you and want to be in your life, they must be willing to also do for you. Secondly, and I believe this whole-heartedly about Harold, that watching his sisters use and lie to men the way that they did, made Harold have a deep distrust and even a sort of hatred for women. Although he disagreed with me, I couldn't help but believe I was right. Whenever we discussed the women that he victimized, or even women in general, Harold would speak of them as if they somehow deserved whatever was done to them. To him, women were all out to get whatever they could out of you anyway, therefore it was better to get them before they got you. He had a hidden disdain for women that I believe he didn't realize he had. He couldn't tell me about one woman that he ever really loved or even treated well.

By his senior year of high school, the last of his sisters had moved out of the house. His mom was still rarely around, so Harold was basically on his own. As he described it, while his friends were playing video games and wasting time doing other stuff teenagers do, he was busy doing man shit, with his focus on surviving and providing for himself. Like his sisters before him, Harold decided early on that it was easier and much more fun to make his way by having someone else pay his way. Harold made it clear to me that as far back as he could remember, he never developed a desire to live any other way.

Harold was always a very handsome kid growing up. And at seventeen, he was well over six feet tall, and had developed into a very attractive young man who would garner attention from women of all ages. By this time, Harold had gotten pretty good at getting girls to do stuff for him as well. Even as a teen, he had a rule that any girl who came over to the house to spend time with him, could not come empty handed. Whether it was food, something to smoke, or some alcohol to drink, the girls would have to come bearing gifts. Harold told me that he had so many girls down with this program, that he never had to worry about buying food for the house. After a while, he graduated to having these girls bring him money whenever he needed it. And once he was able to do that, Harold said for him, there was no turning back.

The first woman that Harold hung out with who had her own place was thirty something year old Barbara. He was still in high school, and he met Barbara when she came to visit her sister and her family who had just moved next door to Harold. She was too old to be messing with a young man his age, so to keep her relationship with Harold a secret from her family, she would pick Harold up from a nearby street corner and take him back to her place. He remembered she wasn't very good looking, and sometimes she was a pain in the ass because she would want to see him all the time. But she always had money that she was cool with spending on him, and a car that she allowed him to drive, despite the fact that he didn't even have a driver's license at the time. All he had to do was give her a good screw whenever she wanted, which at the time was all he had to offer anyway. Harold looked at it as a trade-off. The more she was willing to give him, the more he would make himself available to her. He told me how after he would spend the night at her place, he would drop her off at work the next morning in her car and keep it all day until she got off. He was even using the car and some of the money she was giving him to hang out with other girls, and she didn't have a clue he was doing it.

Then the inevitable began to happen, the more and more time he spent over Barbera's, the less time he spent at home or in school. It got to the point where he stopped going to school all together. When the school finally contacted his mother about his many absences, his mother demanded that he return to school immediately. Unfortunately, Harold had tasted adult life and freedom for too long by that point, and he wasn't willing to give it up, even for his mother. So, when she gave him the ultimatum of returning to school or having to move out of her house, Harold chose to move out, and in with Barbara. And that's where Harold's life as a Hobosexual began, at the age of eighteen.

CHAPTER TWO

How To Spot One

Sub One:

Obvious Red Flags

These are things that should never get pass you:

"He's homeless!"

Any grown person that you meet who doesn't have his own place, or is sleeping on the couch of a friend, you must suspect that something possibly could be wrong with that person. I'm not in any way asserting that all people who are down on their luck and forced to crash with a friend is conmen, I'm simply suggesting that for your own protection, you must treat that individual as if he may be a Hobosexual until you are able to prove that they're not. Hopefully, it will turn out that your new friend isn't one, but until you know for sure, proceed with caution.

If the first time you interact with a dog that you're unfamiliar with, you treat that dog as if that dog will most likely bite, you're less likely to get bitten if he turns out to be a dog who bites. It doesn't mean that you will absolutely not be bitten, it just lowers the chance tremendously. If you meet a person who is currently staying with someone until he can get on his feet, assume he may be trying to get close to you to help get on his feet. This does not make you a bad person, it makes you a cautious person. This doesn't mean you're gonna treat him badly or differently than any other new person that comes into your life. Assuming he possibly is a Hobosexual simply means you're on guard. Assuming it simply means that you're not ignoring the possibility that he could be one. It means because he's homeless, the fact is you don't know, so you're going to treat him accordingly. It means you're on alert, and ready to spot any questionable behavior. If you meet someone and they happen to be without a home of their own, I don't see anything wrong with you making sure they aren't looking to date you so that they can solve that problem. Anytime you meet someone in badly need of something that you have, you must be cognizant of the fact that they may have targeted you for that something.

A person without a place to stay is likely going to be willing to do any and everything to find a place to stay. Not all will stoop to conning and scamming, but most will do almost anything up to conning and scamming to solve that problem. And because there is a small segment of society who will cross that line into conning and scamming, I recommend you treat every homeless person that tries to get to know you like they are a part of that small segment. Again, a strange dog probably won't get the chance to bite you if you treat all strange dogs as if they are out to bite you. My mom used to tell me to be careful around all stray dogs, even if it looks gentle and friendly. I remember her words clearly, "If it has teeth, then it can bite you."

"Broke, but still dating!"

A person who doesn't have a job or money, and no place to stay but still pursues you, needs his intentions to come under question. He has nothing to offer you outside of sex, you on the other hand have so much to offer him. With this being the case, it's essential that you keep this fact in mind as you open yourself up to the idea of allowing him into your life. He has nothing, you have everything. You have money and a home, he has neither of these things. You can instantly solve his problems, while he most likely can only offer you orgasms and a few laughs. You must ask yourself a few questions, "Why does a person with nothing want to pursue a relationship with someone who has everything?" "Why does this person want to move into your home, when he is unable to pay bills where he currently lives?" "Why is this person okay with pursuing a relationship with you when he can't even take care of himself?"

The number one goal of a person who has no place to stay, is or should be to find a place to stay. Being in a relationship with you should have to get in line behind getting a job and becoming financially independent, caring for any children that he may have, and doing all in his power to ensure that this homeless situation doesn't occur again. In my opinion, pursuing and dating you should not even be on the menu. He has so much more important and urgent issues that he should be attending to. And if he seems to be more interested in pursuing a situation with you than solving these issues, at a minimum his sense of responsibility must be questioned. I'll repeat, if you meet someone who doesn't have a place to stay, and you have a place for him to stay, there's nothing wrong with you wanting to make sure that's not the reason he's trying to get close to you.

To be honest, if I was basically homeless, I truly believe any woman that I pursue is likely going to be someone who can help me out of the situation. There's a reason why this man that you have met who is crashing on his friend's couch, isn't pursuing a relationship with a woman who is also sleeping on a friend's couch. For most people who find themselves really struggling in life, finding true love, and saving themselves go hand and hand. It's going to be very difficult for a drowning person to fall in love with someone not able to toss them a life preserver. That's why it's very important that you always question why someone with nothing, is open to pursuing a relationship with you.

"He uses a homebase!"

Because Hobosexuals are constantly on the move, most of them have an address that they use as what I call their "homebase". The homebase is usually a location that he trusts to always be there for him regardless of what happens in his life. The homebase is where he can rely on to have his mail delivered, and the mail will be held there safely until he gets an opportunity to retrieve it. It's usually the home of a loved one, or simply a place where the people living there feels a since of responsibility for the Hobosexual. A person not living at the place in which they receive their mail can be a true sign that the person is someone who is always on the move. If you meet someone who must go somewhere other than where he lives to collect his mail, you need to question the reason why.

To most, this may not be a sign of potential trouble. Who really cares where a person gets their mail delivered, right?! But just because you might not be concerned, doesn't mean you shouldn't be. I can understand how this might not raise an eyebrow for some, because we're just talking about mail. Maybe he has a legitimate reason for having it delivered to an address other than where he stays. There could be a legitimate reason why the person is doing this, just make it your business to find out what that reason is.

Regardless of if he ends up living with you or anywhere else, his homebase will always be recognized as his place of residence. It'll be where he will most likely go when times get too tough for him to handle, like if he's unable to find another person to victimize. His homebase is also the address you'll probably find on his driver's license and any other form of identification he uses. The homebase, as well as the phone number associated with it, is the one aspect of the Hobosexual's life that usually will never change. It's the place where an old associate looking to reconnect with him can go. The Hobosexual Homebase is usually the one and only spot in his life that he can depend on to never let him down.

But one crazy aspect of the Hobosexual's homebase is that the people who live there sometimes won't have a clue of how the Hobosexual is living his life. They may not know that they are acting as a homebase for a loved one who is living as a social conman. Even if it's a member of his family, or his best friend in the world, he or she just may not be aware of how the Hobosexual is surviving. Just like he's conning you, he likely could be conning them as well.

"His first lie!"

"When someone shows you who they are, believe them the first time."

Maya Angelou

Every victim I've ever spoken to always could recall back to the moment they caught their Hobosexual in his first lie. The victims would all go on to regret not ending the relationship at that very moment. They told me how it would have saved them so much financially and emotionally had they cut ties at the first moment of discovering that he was willing to lie. Every victim told me how angry they were with themselves for not acting immediately after catching him in the first tall tale he told. They agreed that the first lie that they all ignored, turn out to be the prelude to many more to come.

The problem is that when most women catch their new man telling a lie, the women may have already started liking the idea of that new man being in their life. She may be enjoying having that attractive and attentive man lying next to her at night. At that point she may be loving the man, so she simply ignores the lie, or accepts any justification that he gives for telling it. If she's really far gone, she may even create her own excuse for him telling the lie.

The first lie you catch a person you've recently met telling you, should be the last lie he ever tells you, simply because they shouldn't get another opportunity to tell another one. You should understand and accept that the moment you catch someone in the first lie, you're dealing with someone who's okay with telling them. You're dealing with someone who is comfortable misleading you. You are now interacting with someone that doesn't respect you, and someone who just might have ulterior motives for being in your life. You should also know that you may be dealing with someone trying to hide something, and he's most likely using lies to do it.

If he'll lie about one thing, he'll surely lie about another. A person who you've recently met should not have a reason to lie to you. And if they do, it usually means that they are doing it for their own personal gain. Why else does a person that you just met have a reason to not be truthful? For your own protection and peace of mind, you must separate yourself from anyone that you find lying, especially a person claiming that they are interested in getting close to you. And if he's interest in moving in with you and you discover he's lying to you, you better run for the hills.

That first lie should place into question everything else that he has told you up to that point, and a red flag should be raised over anything that he tries to tell you after. You must not treat the first lie that you catch as the first one he's told, but instead it's the first one you've caught him telling. Or treat it as the weakest lie, the lie that had the unlikeliest chance of getting pass you. And if that lie was the weakest of his lies, imagine the whoppers that you didn't catch. Lying for a Hobosexual comes as easy as breathing. Lying is essentially how he makes his living, how he eats and keeps a roof over his head. A person who has nothing and who intends to live off you without you becoming aware that he has nothing, must be able to lie very well. He is going to mislead you from the day he meets you, to the day he leaves you. And if he gets one lie pass you, he's gonna tell another, and another, and another.

Sub Two:

What They Look Like?

If you are expecting this duck to look and quack like a duck, you don't know much about this type of duck. And here's why:

"All colors, shapes, and sizes!"

Anyone can be a conman. It doesn't matter what they look like, how old, how dumb, or smart they are. Hobosexuals come in all colors, shapes, and sizes. It's why so many people get dupped and fooled, used, and abused. There's no way of spotting one by just looking at him. The only thing I can tell you for sure is that you won't know what he is, until you discover what he is. Because you won't know until you figure it out. Nothing truly reveals if a person is a Hobosexual except his behavior. His build, the clothes that he wears, his demeanor or mannerisms are not going to tell you anything. He'll look like me, he'll look like you. Just like you won't be able to look at a person and tell if he's a thief, you won't be able to look at someone and tell if he's a social predator. A Hobosexual may have the physique of a man who lives in a gym, just as much as he may have the body of someone who lives on ice-cream and donuts. He could look just as much like a tattooed biker gang member as he does the paster at your church. He has no physical features that would distinguish him from anyone else that you may run into. What makes the Hobosexual a Hobosexual is where he sleeps, and how he gets to sleep there.

And as far as looks are concerned, a Hobosexual must only be attractive and desirable to his victim, not the rest of the world. Of course, it's true that the more attractive he is, the more successful he most likely can be. But because looks are subjective, being good looking is not a requirement. The Hobosexual's number one tool is sex, and luckily for the preservation of mankind, no one must be attractive to use that tool. If there was a way to look at a person and tell if he were a social predator in need of a place to stay, he would most likely remain homeless. Anyone that you meet can be a Hobosexual, anyone, anywhere and at any time.

"They're folks you know!"

Believe it or not, you have not only met a Hobosexual during your lifetime, but there's also a good chance you are currently associated with one, and you just don't know it. It's not a lifestyle that most people are proud of, so don't be surprised that no one that you know will admit to ever being one, or even being victimized by one. Hobosexuals come from the same environments that we all come from. The same neighborhoods, the same cities, the same towns. They're your loved ones, your neighbors, and co-workers. They're people that you grew up with, and surely folks that you come across every day.

He's that friend of yours who seems to get involved with a different woman every few months, if not every few weeks. It's your cousin who every time he changes up girlfriends, he changes up where he lives. It's that buddy who whenever you see him, is always driving a different car, even though you've never known him to own a car of his own. He's your brother or uncle who despite never being able to keep a job, never seems to be short on cash or a place to stay. The Hobosexual is your co-worker who every time you turn around, he's introducing you to a new fiancé, but never ever actually gets married. He's that gym rat who when you go workout, he's there working out. In fact, it seems like he lives at the gym, which he just may. Whether we are aware of it or not, we all most likely know a Hobosexual or two.

Most of the time when a person is living as a Hobosexual, no one he knows actually is aware that he is living that way. Not his mom, not his sister or brother, not even his close friends. Being a Hobosexual wasn't anything that he openly talked about. As far as his loved ones knew, each place where he lived was just somewhere he shared with the woman that he was seeing at that time, and somewhere he shared the bills. You couldn't have known that the woman was basically taking care of him. To those who knew him, his relationship and living situation appeared very normal.

The fact is anybody can be or could have once been a Hobosexual. Rarely does a person live as one all their life. You could meet a person who is living a perfectly normal life now, but was living like a conman the previous year, or even the previous month. You could know someone currently living as a Hobosexual, then just a couple months later, they could be living alone in a home where they pay all the bills. The truth is, unless someone that you know admits to you that they are a Hobosexual, chances are you'll just never know it, unless they attempt to victimize you.

I've personally known at least five men in my lifetime who lived as Hobosexuals during the period in which I knew them. I've known many guys who once lived that way in their past, but it's five men in particular that I knew well as they were actively victimizing the women that they were living with at that time. In most of the occasions when they were living that way, none of our mutual friends had a clue that they were doing it. These guys would live as Hobosexuals just long enough for them to get on their feet, then usually would never return to the lifestyle, so none of our other friends would ever catch on to what they did.

Remember I call it a taboo topic. No one likes to talk about it, especially the people involved. So, if your cousin's girlfriend is keeping her mouth shut, how would you ever know what your cousin ever did to her? If you're neighbor never discusses with you how he's living, how would you ever know he's taking advantage of his roommate that way? How would you ever know your brother-in-law hasn't worked or paid a bill in the house if your sister doesn't admit that with you? How would you find out that the apartment where your co-worker is living is a place where he's just crashing on the couch? You wouldn't know, and you probably wouldn't really have a way of knowing. The fact is, it's highly unlikely that if you are sociable in the slightest that you are not associated with someone who has either been a Hobosexual or is currently living as one.

"He won't look needy!"

If you're expecting a Hobosexual to look homeless or like someone who needs your help, you're going to be greatly disappointed, and likely find yourself being victimized in the future. Although a Hobosexual needs a place to live, he most likely won't look like he does. He may even appear to be someone who can do more for you than you could ever do for him. Remember, a conman is going to look the role that he's trying to play, and a homeless person is not the role that he's trying to pull off.

Think about all the famous cases of people being swindled out of their money. The victims were never scammed by people who appeared to be badly in need of money. Instead, the scammers were always people who their victims thought already was successful and had a lot of money of their own. They also presented themselves to their victims as people who had their best interest in mind. The Hobosexual works in a very similar fashion. He'll initially present himself as a person who is happy and has everything that he already needs. One swindler scam to fill his pockets, while the other scam to gain a place to sleep, and neither's appearance will ever give away their true intentions.

The idea that you can't judge a book by its cover is definitely the case when dealing with a Hobosexual. He won't look like what he is, nor will he appear to live the way he's actually living. His appearance will be just as much a part of his game as the lies he tells. He can't look like a conman, then turn around and try to run a con. The part he wants to play is of a suitable suitor. People are not going to hoodwinked by someone who looks like he hoodwinks people for a living. He'll look like your normal, everyday boyfriend, significant-other, or husband. He'll appear to be hardworking when he's far from it. He'll look like a million bucks when he won't have a penny to his name. He'll seem self-sufficient when he'll need to depend on you for any and everything. So, if you're looking for him to look homeless, you better look again.

"Too good to be true!"

The old saying, "if something appears to be too good to be true, it usually is," is spot on when it comes to dealing with this type of character. As crazy as it may sound, if you were to meet someone that appears to be the perfect potential mate for you, it should instantly cause you to expect that he's not. The more that they go out of their way to make you feel good, the more you need to suspect that they have a hidden agenda that involves making you feel good. I know this seems like a crazy way of treating your seemingly Mister Right, but it's the only way to truly protect yourself from being victimized by a Hobosexual disguised as Mister Right. A Hobosexual is surely going to do his best to appear to be the man of your dreams, when in reality, he's the man of your nightmares.

The Hobosexual believes that the more perfect he can appear to be for you, the less of his character you will scrutinize. The more you're blown away by who he presents himself to be, the more you'll likely disregard the obvious signs that there are issues with his personality, and the more you'll ignore the fact that he doesn't have the ability to back-up much of the claims that he makes.

Remember, the perfect man is that carrot that he's dangling out in front of you in an attempt to sweep you off of your feet. And it's at that very moment when you find yourself swept in the air that you should stop everything and ask yourself a few questions. Like, why is a man that appears to be so perfect, so available? He's perfect, but always available for a new relationship. Why is a person who appears to be a perfect companion for you, therefore most likely perfect for many other women, always single and ready to mingle? If he's supposed to be the man of your dreams, wouldn't he likely be the man of someone else's dreams? Why is a man who represents himself as such a great catch, always available to be caught? Not only pose these questions to yourself, also feel free to ask him the same questions as well.

The next question is usually the most difficult for a person to face, but it's one that can help protect from being victimized. Why me? Why is this perfect man choosing to pursue a relationship with me? What makes me so special? This to-good-to-be-true man can have just about any woman he wants, so why date you? I'm not suggesting that you do an evaluation to measure your self-worth, I'm simply suggesting that you do your best to figure out what is making this perfect man decide to pursue a relationship with you. What distinguishes and separates you from all the other women that also must recognize how great of a catch he appears to be? What things have you shown him in the brief time you've known him that has caused him to be so taken by you? Again, this doesn't mean that you question your worth as a person. You know how great you are, and you should be proud of that person. You just want to ensure that it's actually your greatness that this perfect man is really attracted to.

Sometimes our egos will get us into some deep, deep trouble. And if you have a big ego, as I admittedly do, a skilled Hobosexual will use that big ego against you. A person with a huge ego will hesitate to ask questions such as these, questions that are meant to protect you, not demean you. Pushing aside your ego is a skill that most folks never master. And that's unfortunate, because it can really help you avoid a lot of pain and misery if you can master it. When dealing with a potential threat like a conman, setting aside your ego is skillset that you will definitely want to be able to rely on.

Sub Three:

He's Moving Quickly

Keep out of the way of a speeding car, it usually has a place it's badly needing to get to, and fast.

"Too quick to sleepover!"

Of course, you should be skeptical of anyone who you just recently met and don't know very well, who is eager to spend the night in your home. Why does a man who represents himself as someone who has a place of his own, suddenly after a few days of seeing you, is anxious to now sleep in your bed? Why is he so comfortable doing that? And why is he so comfortable doing that with you? These are the type of questions you must take a moment to ask yourself when meeting someone showing eagerness to spend the night with you.

There is a big difference between having sex with someone in your bed, and someone spending the night in your home. There's a difference between someone being anxious to sleep with you, and someone being anxious to sleep over. The two do not necessarily mean the same thing. And before you allow someone to enter your home, you need to find out which one they're after. You should never conflate the two. Allowing a stranger to sleepover at your place could result in you actually aiding someone who may be out to victimize you. A man who doesn't need a place to sleep does not or should not be so eager to rest in your bed. if he is, the reason for his eagerness must come into question.

Sex does not have to end in a sleepover. When it does, it makes you vulnerable to social predators. A person who has sex with you, basically has access to your body. But a person who has sex with you in your bed, has access to your home and everything inside it. My advice to you would be that you never allow someone that you don't truly know well spend the night in your home for any reason. A man with something of his own, should not need to use something of yours, and that includes your bedroom.

Being easy and fast sexually isn't against the law and neither should it be. If it were, I would have been arrested and thrown behind bars a long time ago. In fact, I would be considered a lifelong career criminal felon on the top of the FBI most wanted list. So, trust me, I'm in no way suggesting that you're somehow less of a person if you're having sex with people soon after you meet them. Allowing them to sleep over is when your judgement comes into question.

If you know that the person you just met is crashing on his friend's couch, and he is eager to spend the night at your place, there could be an agenda behind that eagerness, and you should want to find out what that agenda is. If it's not his agenda that should come under question, maybe it's his judgement. A man who is quickly trying to get you comfortable with him sleeping over could be a sign that he's a man who needs your bed, instead of a man who simply wants to have sex in your bed.

"Too quick to let you pay!"

Be cautious of any person who soon after meeting them, the person is completely comfortable with you spending your money on them. Even if he claims he's not comfortable but still allows you to do it. Pretending to not be comfortable with it is a part of the Hobosexual's game, so you still need to be cautious. Especially considering you don't know them very well. There's nothing wrong with you using your own money to treat someone that you like to a good time, just be aware that if he is cool with you doing it, he may be cool with it because he's a user who needs you to do it. A person that you just meet who has their own money should not need or want you to spend money on them. And if they do, you should want to know why. Also, anyone that you meet, who doesn't have any money of his own but is still eager to date you, is also someone who's character deserves to be scrutinized. This is because a person who doesn't have anything, is usually someone who needs everything.

Too often we get so caught up in the fact that a person wants to be in our lives, that we neglect to want to know why they want to be there. When it's really the why that's much more important than the fact that they simply are there. We place too much focus on what we want from the person we meet, and not enough focus on what that person may want from us. And a person that you just met who is quick to be comfortable with you paying his way, may be someone that you also need to be cautious of.

Until you really know what a person's intentions are, you should not be freely spending money on them. The fact is if you really don't feel you know what their agenda is, you really don't know them. You can't classify someone as your friend if you really don't know why they desire your friendship. It's easy to figure out if a person you've just met does not need your money spent on him, because he'll spend his own. It's quite easy to know if someone you've just met is pursuing you for you, instead of pursuing you for your money, don't allow him access to your money and see if he sticks around. You don't want to associate yourself with someone who as he tells you he likes you and wants to get to know you better, he's happy, if not eager to allow you to spend your money on him.

A friendship or relationship must be based on trust. And how can you trust someone when you don't have a grasp on why they are pursuing a relationship with you? The fact is until you know why he's there, you need to keep him at a distance. If he's fast to let you pick up the check, picking up the check may be why he's there. You need to know if picking up the check is just the beginning, because it could be a sign of a much bigger financial responsibility that he's expecting you to take on.

"Too quick to claim you!"

Remember the Hobosexual doesn't have a lot of time to mess around, he must be a big advocate, believer, supporter of love at first sight. So, if a man that you just met begins to treat you like his girlfriend, or begins to claim you as his lady, you might be dealing with someone that is trying to take advantage of you. You could have just met a man who's desperate for a place to stay. Regardless of you feeling like you've known him all your life after just the second conversation, a man that you've only known a short period of time should not be claiming you as his. There's probably a reason he's making that call so quickly, and it's probably not for the same reason that you enjoy hearing him claim you.

There's a method to his madness. There's a reason he needs you to be identified as his woman, his girlfriend, or his lady. It's because of the position that the title of being your man places him in within your life. It's the privileges and benefits that come along with being your significant other. Being considered your man gives him certain rights, at least in the mind of the Hobosexual. For example, being your man allows him to sleep in your bed, eat your food, or even drive your car without being criticized for doing so. As your man, he can get you to spend money on him without there being any expectation of re-payment. When you're in a relationship, who cares if only one person, you in this case, always pays for the date?! He's your man, so what if you always grab the check?! The position of being your man gives the Hobosexual a built-in excuse for being dependent on you for everything; as well as giving you the justification for fully caring for him.

Another reason the Hobosexual wants to quickly be recognized as your man and to have you recognized as his lady is because he wants to keep the wolves off his back. The wolves being your family and friends. If the two of you can claim being a couple, your loved ones may be a bit reluctant to question why he's living with you rent free. Again, claiming you as his lady allows him certain perks and privileges that being someone you just met would certainly not give him. And the Hobosexual does not need your friends and loved ones in your ear while he's running game. An important title may keep their interference at bay.

Once a Hobosexual can get his victim to be okay with him calling her his lady, there's no longer a need to even ask her can he stay the night, he's expected to. In fact, for many women, he's required to spend the night. I once dated a woman name Tammy who I began sleeping with just days after meeting her. The moment we had sex, she began introducing me to folks as her man. After that, spending the night for Tammy was mandatory, at either her place or mine. For her, the sleep over was as much a part of sex as removing our clothes were. I believe in my heart that Tammy began to quickly call me her man because it justified us basically living at each other's homes very soon after meeting. I really didn't mind her staying over after sex, I just didn't feel comfortable with the label of being her man. I allowed her to do it because it made her comfortable with us sharing so much with each other despite only being together for a short period of time.

If I were lounging around, just hanging out in Tammy's bedroom and a family member or friend of hers stopped by, she would simply tell them that her man was asleep in her bedroom. The fact of the matter is her loved ones didn't know me, so she didn't feel comfortable telling them that "G.L." is asleep in the bedroom. She did this to avoid her loved ones from negatively judging her. And in this way, Tammy's reasoning behind labeling me as her man is very similar to the reasoning behind the Hobosexual labeling his victim as his lady. Tammy used the label to justify our actions together, just as the Hobosexual will use the title to justify his actions with you. Although the agenda is different, the reason behind Tammy and a Hobosexual's actions were nearly identical.

You must be suspicious of anyone who claims you as theirs really quick after meeting them. What's behind them doing it? Do they have an ulterior motive? Why are they moving so fast, what's their end game? Like I said before, a man who just enters your life and really hasn't gotten to know you should not be making a claim of you, nor should you be making a claim of him. Being just your friend, your date, a homeboy or even a lover, doesn't empower him the way he needs and wants these terms to empower him. These terms keep him weak and makes his position in your life too insignificant. In a way, these terms may render him powerless.

Instead of being enamored with the fact that he's calling you his lady, what perks that come with that title is he taking advantage of? Two days after meeting you he's calling you his boo, soon after that, he's asking to borrow cash. Or the day after he began referring to you as sweetie, he asked to use your car. He calls you his Lady and the next thing you know he's showing up at your door with an overnight bag. Once you hear the intimate title being used, keep an eye out for the favor request that comes after. The game behind the claims will easily reveal itself if you just keep an eye open for it.

Unfortunately, what normally happens with most women is that they get so excited with suddenly being claimed by a new man, that they become unable to see the obvious signs that there could be a problem with that new man. Especially if the victim is desperate for companionship, she may not be mentally capable of recognizing the game that a conman is playing. In fact, she may not even want to recognize his game. She may be so desperate for love, that she would rather risk the possibility of him being a user, than she would want to risk losing him. The fact that a man is claiming her so quickly may move her so much, that she would never question why he's so quick to do so.

"Too quick to claim your stuff, as his stuff!"

He's basically a homeless conman, therefor he must act fast. He's up against the gun, he has no time to waste. One way you may know that a man you just met is a Hobosexual is how fast he tries to get to be able to claim not only you, but your stuff as his own. He'll quickly and methodically begin using terms such as ours, we, us, together, or couple. Your friends quickly become his friends, or our friends, your family suddenly becomes his family. Your favorite restaurant becomes our favorite restaurant. And believe it or not, your money will quickly become our money.

In a blink of an eye, a skilled Hobosexual will make your world his own. You probably won't even notice it until it happens. Before you know it, your friends will be including him on friendly outings. He'll do his best to connect with your close relatives so that he's invited to family get-togethers. I've not only seen it happen, but I've experienced it firsthand. He'll begin claiming your world and everything inside it as his. Instead of asking to borrow your car, it'll be "the" car that's he's asking to use. Soon after that it'll be "our" car. Before you know it, your new man will be driving your car just as much, if not more often, than you do. He'll be dropping you off at work, and you won't see your car until it's time for him to pick you back up. To many of his friends, your car will be recognized as his car. I once knew a dude who soon after he started living with a woman, he not only began driving her car, but he actually customized her car the way he wanted it to look. He replaced the rims and tires, he upgraded the stereo, he even tinted the windows. The car instantly went from being her car, to his car almost overnight. The only time you even saw her in the car was when he transported her back and forth to work so that she could keep up with the car payments. Eventually, she had to ask him if she could drive her own car when she needed to.

The quicker the Hobosexual can make your stuff his stuff, the quicker he can start using your stuff whenever he wants. The quicker he can call your bed his bed, and the sooner it can become a normal thing for him to be sleeping in it. He needs to quickly have your home and everything in it to be recognized as his own. He needs to convince you to accept him claiming it as his own so that he can freely use it at his leisure. Claiming your stuff very quickly is also a wonderful way of gauging your feelings and attitude toward him. It's a good way to measure just how strong of a position he holds in your life. If you complain about him claiming your stuff as his own, he knows he has more work to do. If you have a problem with him making these claims, he knows that he doesn't have enough control over your heart the way he needs to have. The more he can claim, the stronger the position he maintains in your life, as well as in your bed.

The Story of Marcus
"The Carrot Dangler"

The year 2009 was a really bad time for my friend Marcus. He had hit rock bottom. At only twenty-nine years old, he found himself divorced, unemployed, and living back in his mother's basement. He was also struggling with a very serious alcohol problem. All of that, along with his ex-wife and children not wanting anything to do with him, had sent Marcus into a deep depression. To make matters worse, his days of living rent free with his mother was soon coming to an end. Like I said, it just wasn't a good time for Marcus.

To truly understand how and why Marcus ended up this way, you must really get to know more about him. His father died when he was about eight years old, and he grew up the only child of an overprotective and overbearing mother. After losing her husband, Marcus's mom's life became all about Marcus, and she spoiled him the way you would expect most widowed young mothers with no other family would. He was the apple of his mother's eye. I really don't remember Marcus being able to do anything without it being under the watchful eye of his mom. He wasn't even allowed to walk to school like the rest of us, even though the school was less than a couple of blocks outside of our neighborhood. His mom dropped him off and picked him up all the way up to his second year of high school. And boy did he catch hell from the other kids for that.

This babying of Marcus continued on even after he graduated. His mother brought him a car, provided him with money, and she even transformed the basement of her home into a Marcus bedroom/ man-cave. I believe she did all of this so that Marcus wouldn't have an incentive to leave her. She didn't require him to get a job, nor did he have to give any thought about his future; all Marcus was required to do was continue being her little boy, even though he was far, far from being a little boy. She just wanted him home with her, and she was willing to do whatever it took to keep him there. And I believe Marcus was taking full advantage of that.

Even though he was well into his twenties, Marcus had it made in the shade. He had no reason or incentive to get a job, he spent his time in that basement playing video games and hanging out drinking with his friends. His favorite past time was chasing after women which he spent much of his days and nights doing. He didn't have a worry in the world. And if he ever did, his mother was there to help rid him of that worry. Marcus was living the good life, he had everything and anything that he wanted at his beck and call. That is until his mother met a new beau, married that new beau, then moved her new hubby in the house with her and Marcus. And it was at that point that everything began to change for my friend. And I don't mean for the better. When Marcus's new stepdad, Mr. Jake, arrived, Marcus's free ride in his mother's house began coming to an end.

Mr. Jake wasted no time taking over as head of the house, and he and Marcus began clashing right out of the gate. Mr. Jake was an old school retired military man, very stern, who would never accept a grown man living at home and still being cared for by his mother. Which unfortunately described Marcus perfectly. Marcus sitting around playing video games all day, not working but still able to come and go as he pleased was a serious issue for his mother's new husband. Mr. Jake had already raised two sons with his ex-wife. And like their father, both his sons' pursued careers in the military soon after high school. So needless to say, from day one, Mr. Jake had Marcus square in his crosshairs.

Mr. Jake made it clear to both Marcus and his mother, Marcus had to either start getting his shit together, or he had to move out, period and no negotiating. And to Marcus surprise as well as to his disappointment, his mother was backing whatever decision or play her new husband made. Whenever Marcus and Mr. Jake had a disagreement, which occurred almost daily, she always sided with her new husband regardless of which of the two men was in the wrong. When it got to the point where the situation in the house was becoming very volatile, Marcus packed his things and moved in with Karen, one of the girls he was seeing at the time who had her own apartment. And within that same year, Karen discovered she was pregnant, and the two later marry just before the child is born.

In the beginning, married life for Marcus was just like living in his mom's basement. Karen paid all the bills, Marcus spent most of his time playing video games and hanging out with his buddies. As far as jobs went, he would occasionally work, the problem was he was so inconsistent with it that it was difficult to call it really ever working at all. Whenever he would grow tired of Karen complaining about having to carry all the couple's financial weight, Marcus would get a job for about a month or two, then quit or get fired for showing up late or sometimes not showing up at all. Marcus spent more time unemployed during his marriage than he ever did employed. And this caused the two of them to really struggle financially, placing a heavy load on the shoulders of his young wife.

Even after Karen gave birth to their daughter, Marcus nonchalant attitude toward working didn't change. In fact, it got worse. So did his drinking, and so did his partying and spending time outside the home in an attempt to avoid Karen's complaining. When he would return, he would usually be too drunk to even carry on a conversation with his wife. The more the bills began to pile up, the more of a problem Karen had with him not bringing in any money. For the first time in his life, Marcus was faced with having to step up as a man. Unfortunately, this was a step Marcus was unable, and unwilling to take.

The struggling continued as the years went by. Even after Karen gave birth to their second child, Marcus just wouldn't change his ways. The more Karen nagged and complained, the more drinking he would do. Trying to keep the family afloat, Karen ended up taking on a second job at night, which was a problem because it was tough getting Marcus to stay home in the evenings to watch the children. The family's struggles got so bad that she had to begin borrowing money from not only her parents, but Marcus's family as well. Even with that, Marcus refused to change.

His drinking eventually became so bad, that he was very seldom seen sober, he had become a serious alcoholic. And that made it impossible for him to keep a job even at times when he would try to. Karen came to resent him for the drinking and lack of responsibility that he showed for his family. Their normal shouting matches began to turn violent. Karen began to actually fear for her own safety. And if that wasn't bad enough, it got to the point if he wasn't home fighting with Karen, Marcus was out spending time with other women, sometimes not returning home for days at a time.

The last straw for Karen was when Marcus, after disappearing on the family for nearly a week, suddenly shows up at home not only drunk, but high on drugs. When Karen confronted him, Marcus assaults her so badly, she ended up in the hospital with a black eye and bruises all over her body. One of the children was also reported to have been injured in the melee. he was arrested, later convicted of domestic abuse against his family and sentenced to one year in jail. While locked up, Karen divorced him, took the kids, and moved to North Carolina where she had family. As a condition to his conviction, Marcus was ordered to never go near Karen or the kids without court supervision.

Marcus did his year, and when he got out, he had nothing and no place to go. And that's how in 2009, a depressed and unemployed alcoholic with nothing to his name, ended up back in his mother's basement. He was there for just about a year before I got wind of what was going on with him. I was living in Los Angeles at the time, and I was back in my hometown Baltimore to visit my family. A friend that Marcus and I grew up with came to see me and filled me in on the latest neighborhood gossip. After this friend caught me up on everything, which included what was going on with Marcus, I decided to visit Marcus to see if there was anything that I could do to help him. So, I shot around to his mom's house, which was still just around the corner from mine.

But the thought of visiting Marcus presented an uncomfortable situation for me to say the least. I hadn't seen nor even talked to him in over six to seven years. After hearing about how bad he was doing, I really didn't know how receptive he was going to be with reconnecting with me. But I still considered Marcus my friend, and if I was able to possibly help him in any way, I had to at least give it a shot. When I got to his mom's house, she informed me that he was no longer living there. He had actually moved out just a few weeks prior to me arriving in town. Although she wasn't exactly sure where he was staying, she suspected he was living with a new girlfriend. His mom told me she'd pass my phone number on to him next time they talked.

I must admit, I was a bit relieved. Marcus must had put all that foolishness behind him if he was now living on his own with a girlfriend. And although the alcohol addiction and stories of abuse surprised the hell out of me, him having a new girlfriend did not. Marcus always did have a way with the ladies. He might not have been able to keep a job, but you could always count on him keeping a woman in his life. So again, I was very relieved to hear he seemed to be back on his feet, and out of his mom's basement. In fact, after speaking with his mother, I no longer had a desire to link back up with him. I simply returned to visiting with my family, forgetting all about Marcus. That is until two days later, I received a call from a Maryland number that I didn't know. But when I answered the call, I instantly recognized the voice on the other end as it yelled, "G-Money!" It was the nickname Marcus gave me way back in kindergarten.

Marcus and I talked on the phone for over an hour, mostly about the days growing up in the old neighborhood. As always, at times, he had me laughing so hard I would almost pee my pants. He always was one of the funniest cats I had ever known. I used to tell people that despite working in comedy in Hollywood for over a decade, I had met very few people that could match his wit and sense of humor. Regardless of everything that I heard he had gone through, it appeared as if it didn't affect his funny bone one bit. As far as I was concerned, it was the same Marcus that I had known since first grade.

I couldn't get over the fact that the guy I was talking to could be the same person who I had heard so many horrible things about. The person I was talking to sounded like he was on top of the world. He had no complaints, and he definitely didn't appear to need any help from me. In fact, He insisted he was having the time of his life, that he was happier than he had been in many, many years. Marcus couldn't stop bragging about how great things were going for him.

I was completely confused, but very happy at the same time, for this was absolutely not the Marcus that I was expecting to hear from. Then he blew my mind even further when he told me he was not only now engaged to a great lady that he was living with, but he was also actually looking forward to getting married again. I was so proud of my friend, who appeared to have withstood the storm and came out on the other side a better man. It seemed as if he had turned his life around, and I was very happy for him. We had such a great time on the phone, that we decided to get together and catch up some more later that same evening.

As always when I visit back home, I usually stay with my sister, and that's where Marcus picked me up. He pulled up in a nice newer model BMW, much better than anything that I was expecting him to be driving. Especially since during our earlier phone call that day, he told me how he was currently in between jobs. When he got out of the car, I instantly noticed his weight loss, which I attributed to the drinking and drug use. We spent a short time hanging out with my family before heading out.

It was around 8pm when we arrived at the lounge that Marcus chose to take me to. I remember it was karaoke night, and the crowd was just showing up as we got there. Soon after we were seated, Marcus made it clear that he was paying for everything. Knowing he wasn't working at the time, I tried my best to pay but he was insisting that the evening be on him. After seeing the big wad of cash he pulled from his pocket, it appeared to me that he may have had more money on him than I had on me. Once the waitress dropped off the first round of drinks, I couldn't hold back any longer, I jumped right in with questions I badly needed answers to. Questions about his divorce, his drug and alcohol use, losing his family, as well as how he got back on his feet so damn quickly. To my surprise, Marcus was more than happy to satisfy my curiosity. And the story that Marcus went on to share, blew me away.

He began by admitting how he no longer had any contact with his ex-wife and young children. They basically had disowned him. Although he had no problem telling me about it, I had already known about the order of protection that his wife had filed against him. But what Marcus told me that I didn't already know, was that he had been arrested a few times for assaulting his wife before she finally divorced him. He also told me how he had lost his license to drive due to a couple of DUI convictions, which I found strange because he had picked me up for our dinner date. Marcus also confessed that alcohol wasn't the only substance that he struggled with. And although he didn't specify what his drug of choice was, nor did I ask him, I suspected by the way he looked that it had to have been cocaine. In the neighborhood in which we grew up, it was the drug of choice and the one easiest to get your hands on.

He told me that it was in jail where he actually first hit rock bottom, He had lost everything while there. When he got out, he had no choice but to move back into his mother's home. There, he spent most of his time getting drunk off of the alcohol that his mother bought for him, and indulging in his new favorite past time, socializing online. As he began telling me about all the fun that he's found in messing around on the internet, I began to realize that it wasn't hard work or therapy that helped him get back on his feet, it was online dating that did it.

Marcus found that despite when he was going through some really hard times, when socializing online, he could be whoever and whatever he wanted to be. Online with people who lived outside the neighborhood, Marcus didn't have a drug or alcohol problem, he wasn't unemployed and basically penniless. But rather "Online Marcus" could pretend to be whoever he wanted to be, instead of who he really was. Fortunately, as well as unfortunately for Marcus, he also found that pretending to be a healthy and productive member of society, was quicker and easier than actually becoming a healthy and productive member of society. Online, he had the ability to improve himself, without truly having to improve himself.

Hanging out on the internet for Marcus initially started out as just a way to keep tabs on his estranged ex-wife and children. Because he was ordered by the court to not have any contact of any kind with them, occasionally scanning his ex's social media pages was the only way to see what they were up to. He created a fake account on Facebook and befriended his ex to gain access to her private page. Online, Marcus went by the name "DJ Summers," the nickname of a real person that he and his wife attended high school together. His ex-wife just wasn't aware that DJ Summers was doing time in prison, so he knew she would accept any friend request from DJ. From there, he was able to stalk her without her having a clue he was doing so.

Soon Marcus learned that it wasn't just his ex-wife he could fool online. He realized he could fool just about anyone, especially unsuspecting women who were desperate to meet men to date. He expanded his online presence from social media pages to dating sites and even meet-up chat rooms, all under the name DJ Summers. Within a short period of time, Marcus was not just interacting with women on these sites, he began hooking-up and having sex with many of them. Well, DJ Summers was.

Afterwhile, hooking up with these women wasn't just about sex for Marcus, it became a way to get his mother and stepfather off of his back. His stepdad wanted him out of the house, so he would use these women as a way of doing just that. He would meet someone online, convince her to come pick him up, and he'd stay with her as long as she'd keep him. It usually would be just for a couple of nights of sex, then the women would simply drop him back off at home. And he had become very good at making this type of thing happen. These women not only didn't mind taking him back to their place for a good time, but they would also feed him and spend money on him as well. This was good for Marcus because outside of the cash his mother was sneaking by Mr. Jake to give him, he didn't have a dime to his name at that time.

Marcus admitted to me that he wasn't interested in getting into a relationship with any of the women, he just really liked what they were able and willing to do for him. None of them really knew anything about him, and if a woman started asking too many questions, he'd simply stop dealing with her and move on to the next one. Marcus had a rule to not deal with a woman for too long. He found that if he just got in, got what he needed and got out as fast as he could, it lowered the risk of his lies being exposed.

But Marcus spending time out of the house wasn't enough for Mr. Jake, he wanted Marcus gone. Mr. Jake's feelings were, if Marcus had the money to be out dating, he should have had money to help pay bills, which of course Marcus was not interested in doing. So, after the two men bumped heads a few more times, with one occasion ending in near fisticuffs, Mr. Jake kicked Marcus out for good. Marcus found himself homeless. Well, not quite homeless. Because it was then that Marcus revealed to me how he had been living ever since his stepdad changed the locks on him.

Marcus had a handful of women he was seeing at the time who each had a place of their own, so he would basically go from one woman's home, directly to another woman's home. Sometimes the women would unknowingly drop him off on the next woman's doorstep, thinking the doorstep was to the home that belonged to a family member where Marcus claimed to be living. Or he would drive one woman's car to go spend time at another woman's house. Marcus had his con game running real smoothly. He had no job, no money, barely clothes on his back, but was able to weave together a circuit of situations that kept a roof over his head without him having to spend a dime. It really surprised me how he was able to make each of these women believe that he was in love and wanted to be in a relationship with them. And with these women believing this falsehood, he could convince them to do almost anything he wanted them to do, including allowing him to periodically claim their homes as his own. Like his fiancé Dawn who he was living with during that time he and I linked back up, who also owned the BMW he was driving that night. Dawn was his second fiancé that he had lived with within the last six months.

Dawn, a single mother of an eight-year-old boy, was the perfect target for Marcus. Her child's father wasn't around, she was alone, and had very little family and friends. To make it even easier for Marcus, Dawn had a self-esteem problem due to being very over-weight. At the time that he met her on a popular online dating site, Dawn was very desperate to meet Mister

Right. She also wanted badly to bring a good father figure into her son's life. Like a lot of women in her position, desperation led her to open her heart, front door, and bed to a man like Marcus.

Marcus weaved perfect stories to justify or hide all the dysfunction and problematic issues that was occurring in his life. To the naked eye, the stories he told appeared legitimate. And Dawn, like the others, ate those stories up like a fat kid with a bag of chips. The stories would make certain aspects of Marcus's life make sense. His lie about his family owning a construction business gave him the ability to justify not having to go to work every day. It allowed him to be free to see the women that he was victimizing whenever he wanted to, and to sleep over without having to report in to work the next morning. He would always claim that his car was in the shop, or that he was allowing a family member like his mom to use his car. He would justify not having any money by claiming his cash was tied up in some new business venture that he and the family was pursuing. He had a lie and excuse for everything. And he was able to get away with these lies and excuses because he really would never stay with a woman long enough for her to catch on to the game he was running.

Although Marcus looked to be doing better in his life, in my opinion he wasn't. He was still drinking heavily, and after spending just a short time with him that night, I suspected that he was also still using drugs. Despite a pocket full of cash, he was still technically broke. He would always have money for some quick fun like drinks with an old friend, but never enough money to pay a bill or two somewhere he was living. Also, any cash that he would have at that time, was totally dependent on the generosity of his victims. All it would take for his whole world to come crashing down on top of his head, was for a couple of these women to catch on to the game that he was playing.

That night I spent with Marcus was the last time I ever spoke with my friend. Over those drinks that night, I so badly wanted to tell him that the way he was living was not going to end well for him. I could see where all the dysfunction, lies and conning were going to take him. But Marcus was only interested in the today, tomorrow was too far out for him to be concerned about. Having a place to lay his head and some money in his pocket, all without having to work, was enough for him to feel like a complete success. I really don't believe I could have said anything that night that could have changed his mind about that.

I not only left the restaurant feeling sorry for the women he was conning, but I also felt sorry for Marcus. He was destroying his life, while in the process of destroying the lives of others. And because he was so caught up in surviving, he just couldn't see the damage that he was causing. That night as he dropped me back off at my sister's and I watched as he drove away, I couldn't help but think to myself that my childhood friend was setting himself up for a life of pain and misery. The Marcus that I once knew no longer existed. The person who had taken his place was on a fast track to take a big fall, and I could see it as clear as day.

Marcus went on living with Dawn for over a year before she finally realized what she had moved into her home. Apparently like I suspected, Marcus was still drinking heavily and using drugs, and unfortunately began exhibiting the same violent behavior he showed with his estranged family whenever he got drunk and high. He began abusing Dawn mentally as well as physically. He also was occasionally stealing from her and disappearing with her car for days at a time. After Dawn received one black eye too many, she kicked him out of her home. But like the true social predator that he had become, Marcus simply moved in with another woman he met online and continued on as if nothing had happened.

Marcus had become a Hobosexual. To be very specific, he had become what I call a Carrot Dangling Hobosexual. Marcus was dangling the idea of a long-term relationship out in front of victims to keep them under his spell. He had no problem disappearing from a woman's life, in the midst of the woman making wedding plans. He also had developed a bad habit of stealing from his women to support his drug and alcohol use. When I initially went by his mom's house looking for him, I recall her asking me if I knew a DJ Summers, because a few women as well as the police had come to her home in search of someone by that name. And neither the women nor the cops were in a particularly good mood. Marcus's mom didn't have a clue that they were actually looking for her son.

Many years had passed since my visit with Marcus over drinks that night. From my understanding, he continued scamming women for quite a while after I last saw him. He was eventually arrested again for domestic abuse, theft by credit card, as well as a few other petty crimes linked to the lifestyle he was leading. After spending some more time in and out of jail, he was back on the street, homeless again. If the stories I've heard over the years are correct, Marcus ended up addicted to heroin, and dying of a drug overdose on his thirty-fourth birthday. RIP my old friend.

CHAPTER THREE

How They Do What They Do

Sub One:

He's All Make-Believe

Like a magician, you gotta assume when he's performing, everything that he does is part of the show.

"He lies for a living!"

You know how you can tell he's telling you a lie? It's easy, his mouth is open. As far as lying goes, there's few better than a Hobosexual. Better than a suspect trying to beat a murder charge, better than a jacked-legged preacher. Hobosexuality and lying goes hand-in-hand. They're the best I've ever heard of. They have to be, they're livelihood literally depends on it. Having a roof over their heads, food in their stomachs and clothes on their backs, is totally dependent on their ability to tell a convincing tale, supporting that tale, and maintaining that tale. He's fake, a figment of his own creation. His past is all make-believe stories created to manipulate you in some form or fashion. The slimiest politician who's up for reelection doesn't have anything on the manipulative ability of a Hobosexual.

Once you discover a person who is living with you is a Hobosexual, you must then question everything that he's ever told you, everything that he's ever done for you. Some of them don't have the ability to be truthful about anything. It's why some truly can't prosper living as a normal member of society because they are sociopathic in that way. The truth is likely going to be a hindrance for him, it's something he doesn't have the time or luxury of utilizing. Remember, the main goal of the Hobosexual is to convince you to let him live in your home rent free for as long as he can, and to get out of there before you discover you've been suckered. Lying gets him from point A to point B, much faster and easier than telling the truth ever will. Telling you what you want to hear, instead of telling you the truth increases his success rate tremendously.

Many people can lie, but most get caught in their lie because of their inability to live the lie. The Hobosexual must not only convince you to believe the lie, but he must also become the lie that he tells. For example, he can't just lie to you about being educated, he must present himself as an educated man when interacting with you. He must walk the walk and talk the talk of an educated man. He must create a background of a person who is educated. The Hobosexual must create a history of education that is believable. Where he attended school, his field of study, when he graduated. He has to not only create his fake history, but he also must be able to convince you that he lived that fake history. Lies to a Hobosexual is what investment capital is for a person in business. It's not only how they both get their new business up and running, but it's also how they maintain it. The lies he tells lay the foundation for which everything else is built on. His lies must be intriguing and attractive, while at the same time very believable and convincing. The lies he tells must not require a lot of physical support. He can't tell you he is rich because it would be very difficult for him to support that lie. But he could tell you that he is working on a business venture that he expects to make him rich, and he may be able to weave together enough lies to support that claim.

The Hobosexual uses lies the same way a spider uses its web. He not only uses it to attract prey, but he also uses it like a spider to trap his prey. But unlike the spider, the Hobosexual's intricate web of lies can be custom baited to attract a specific woman that he has targeted. If she has children, he'll create a web of lies detailing his love and life-long dream of one day fathering children of his own. His sticky trap may be filled with fables of how badly he wants to be a family man, how much he loves children and how great he gets along with them. The web of lies he customizes for that victim just may be a bit too much for her to resist.

Misleading you is how he makes a living. And your ability to recognize a lie when you hear one will not keep you safe when dealing with a very skilled social predator. You won't stand a chance. You'll hear me repeat the following statement often within this project, because it's very important that you understand it:

"His ability to lie is much greater than any skill that you may think you have for being able to recognize a lie. "

You're no match for him, so don't try to be. By the time you do catch him telling you one, he's already gotten a hundred lies by you.

"Just a sprinkle of truth!"

The key for his success is to mix a few small truths on top of and around the big lies that he tells. Just enough truths that if under pressure to prove the big lie is real, he'll simply concentrate on proving that the sprinkled-on truths are legit. Like if a Hobosexual tells you that he attended a very prestigious university, when in actuality he worked there briefly as a janitor. Or instead of attending the school, he actually had a family member graduate from the school. He'll know enough about the university from cleaning it, that he will be able to support his lie of once attending it. He'll have just enough truth intertwined inside the lie that it can make the lie difficult to prove false.

A skilled conman will sprinkle just enough on top of his lie with the belief that if he can prove the 30% of truth that was sprinkled in, you may be inclined to believe the other 70% of bullshit that he cannot back-up. He tells you he's ex-law enforcement, and because he seems very knowledgeable about the law, you believe every word. When in reality, he knows the law well because he's been on the wrong side of it for most of his life. He's never been a cop, he's just been arrested by cops so many times he's probably better at their job than they are. He'll show you a beautiful home in a really nice neighborhood and tell you that he once lived there, leaving out the part of the story that it's the home of one of his previous victims. Like I said, lies with a bit of truth sprinkled on top.

In some cases, instead of adding in a bit of truth, the Hobosexual will instead remove the bad tasting sprinkles from on top of the larger disgusting truth he's telling you. It's a way of lying by omission in an attempt of making a bad tasting truth about himself more attractive for your eating pleasure. If he were to tell you the whole truth and nothing but, you may be inclined not to want to date him. So, he'll still tell you a truth about himself but he's going to keep out all the bad stuff that's mixed in and around that truth. He's being open and truthful about his life, without really being truthful and open about his life. Revealing to you just enough truths about himself that you feel you're dealing with an honest man. Like if he admits to you that he's served time in jail before. But instead of telling you the truth that he was incarcerated for cashing stolen checks or assault, he tells you that it was for overdue parking tickets or driving on a suspended license. He'll replace the more devious crimes that may be a deal breaker for most women, with lighthearted ones that don't in any way make him appear to be such a bad person. He may admit to you that he's divorced. But he won't tell you that his wife left him because he was a horrible human being, instead he'll tell you that he divorced his wife because he found out she was cheating on him. He's being truthful with you, while at the same time omitting bad tasting facts.

"It's everything you want to hear!"

He and his life will be as attractive to you as he can possibly make it. Why waste time trying to get you to like the real him, when simply masquerading as all that you're looking for is much easier? Fooling you into believing he's the one for you takes much less effort. A friend once told me that it was easier to tell someone the truth than it is to tell them a lie. Under most circumstances I tend to agree with this belief. But when living as a Hobosexual, telling the truth can be an occupational hazard. For him, it's easier and less time consuming to simply tell you what you want to hear, instead of actually providing you with what you really want. He doesn't have time for her to learn to like him, he needs her to fall for him almost instantaneously. He can't wait until she comes around to realize he's the man of her dreams, he needs her to believe that soon after she meets him.

Presenting himself as the perfect man that he believes a victim wants in her life is the trick-of-his-trade. In the eyes of his potential victim, he must be as close to her Mister Right as he possibly can be. If she is looking for a man to love and cherish her, that's exactly what he's gonna make her believe he's capable and willing to do. If she needs a man to be a great father figure for her children, he's going to present himself as the perfect stepdaddy. For a woman searching for a man who likes to snuggle in bed while watching romantic films, the Hobosexual is gonna be a person who snuggles and is a fan of romantic films. He's gonna be exactly what she's looking for.

He must be a Jack-of-all-trades. He has to be able to relate to you on whatever level you need him to relate to you on. He's going to be a clean canvas for his victim's personality to create on. What you say, will translate to what he'll be. The first sign that you're dealing with a Hobosexual is the easiest one to spot, it's the sign of the perfect man. The man that you meet, and you instantly believe is perfect, is likely a man who's far from it, and is pretending to be.

There's no perfect man out there. Every person has flaws, every person is going to have traits about them that you're not going to like. Some will have personality traits that you may be a bit too uncomfortable with and not willing to tolerate. But it's these traits that makes us different from one another, they make us who we are, they make us unique and special. A person that you meet who appears to not have any flaws, is likely hiding huge flaws. He has to trick you into believing he's superman, when in reality, he isn't even a good Clark Kent.

Someone who is attempting to con you cannot afford to exhibit any behavior that may make you uncomfortable. He's not looking for you to get to know him better, he's looking to get you to fall for him. And you must be able to understand the difference in the two goals. Someone trying to get you to know them better will be willing to risk showing you the good and bad that comes along with who they are. While someone who is trying to simply win you over will show you only what he believes will impress you. In this case, he's only going to reveal the things about himself that he thinks greatly improves his chances of gaining access to your heart and wallet.

His ultimate goal is to make you fall in love with the person he has created, the make-believe person that he's confident you will be willing to share your home with. He's not looking for a long-term meaningful relationship, he's looking for a place to sleep. And he needs to achieve this right away. But please remember, the more perfect he appears, the more investigating you need to do because that seemingly perfect persona could be the disguise for a really bad human being. That great man that you think you've met could likely turn out to be a man that you'll wish that you've never known.

"He's a top-notch actor!"

It's hard enough to create a new identity, but can you imagine the difficulty of maintaining that identity with someone that you're living with? You would have to be a hell of an actor. You gotta be able to live the lies you've convinced your victim into accepting as truth. It's like living as an undercover agent, you're essentially playing make-believe. You know who you are, but whenever you're around the person who you're living with, you must always be the person that they've gotten to know and fallen in love with. Again, you would have to be one hell of an actor.

A conman not only has to talk the talk, but he also must walk the walk, even when he isn't really walking it. Regardless of how outlandish or farfetched the lie told, he must be able to in some way back it up. Blowing his cover, or as they say in Hollywood, breaking character, could result in him not having a place to sleep. So, the performance that he's gonna likely give will be outstanding. But unlike the Hollywood actor who only has to remain in character until the director yells cut, the Hobosexual can never relinquish the character that he has chosen to play. He's the actor, writer, director, and producer all rolled up in one. And he must perform all of these jobs as close to perfection as he possibly can.

The acting role that the Hobosexual must play is totally dependent on the desires of the woman that he is attempting to manipulate. He may have to play a God-fearing man if his victim is a religious person. He could have to play an educated or sophisticated individual if the victim wants a mate who is educated or sophisticated. It could be one of a neat freak if he moves in with a woman who requires that her home is always neat and clean. If his victim has children, playing a nurturing and loving stepfather isn't difficult for a skilled Hobosexual if the role calls for it.

Needless to say, he has a lot to lose if he were to give a bad performance. One slip-up, and his life instantly changes. He not only has to be great, but he also must be consistently great. One deviation from the script, and all that he's invested in winning you over is lost. If he's committing crimes while he's running his con, he could end up in prison if he doesn't perform well. The show that he puts on has to come off without a glitch. He's likely to be a liar, a cheat, and a thief who is trying to masquerade as the perfect mate for you. It's going to take a hell of an acting job to pull that off.

Sub Two:

They're Skilled At What They Do

When your life depends on you being good at something, you're likely to become great at it!

"He needs to be an asset!"

In order for his game to really work, the Hobosexual needs to convince you that he is a big asset to your life, maybe even that you can't live without him. The more he can get you to believe this, the easier time he'll have getting you to ignore things like him not working, not having money, or not having his own transportation. The more you feel you need him in your life, the more you are compelled to share with him. How can you deny a man money or a place to sleep if you believe in your heart that without him, your life won't function properly? A woman who thinks she can't live without a man will do almost anything to keep him.

He needs you to believe his presence is contributing to your life and household. Especially since he's not capable or even interested in contributing monetarily to it. He has to figure out a way of making his mere presence invaluable. He must and most likely will find a way to convince you that despite all the extra burden that he brings, him just being there makes up for it all. The key to success for him is to raise his value so high, that you don't dare let him go. He must make himself such an asset to your home, that it may not work properly if he isn't living there. At least he must make you believe that this is the truth.

Not able or willing to contribute to your home financially, he may do his best to become sort of a personal assistant to you, someone who makes your life, home or even your business run a bit smoother. He'll try to convince you that you actually benefit from him staying home while you work and pay all the bills. He's there to receive any packages that may need to be signed for. With him there on your couch, you won't have to take off from work when a repairman needs to stop by. You'll even have a live-in maid that's there to ensure you return to a nice clean home after a long day at the office.

If you are a mother with young children, he'll make you feel like he is a Godsend. You'll have a live-in babysitter who works for free. You'll not only save a ton of money, but you'll also have the peace of mind knowing that your kids are in the hands of someone who you believe cares for them as if they're his own. Now instead of having to race from work to pick your kids up from school or daycare, you have a man to do all of that for you. Now you can go about the rest of your day knowing your kids are safe and sound. And when you finally do arrive at home, they've been fed, their homework is done, and they're ready for bedtime. What single mother wouldn't love for this to be her reality?

The stronger the bond a Hobosexual has with his victim, the more successful he can be. The stronger the bond, the more control and power over the victim he has, the more he can get away with. A woman simply wanting a man to live with her may not be a powerful enough emotion for her to have for him, to influence her to put up with a man's Hobosexual behavior. Simple desire isn't a strong enough feeling to make her ignore the fact that a man is unemployed and not contributing at all financially. To get away with all that most Hobosexuals want to get away with, he needs her to badly need him, he needs her to have love for him. He needs her to feel like she can't live without him. The goal is to get his victim to become dependent on him as much as possible. The victim depending on him is the best way to cement his position in her home.

The goal behind everything that he does is to create an unbreakable bond between the two of them, and then take advantage of that bond as best as he can, as quickly as he can. Getting a woman to simply like you, or to simply want you in her life, can get you pretty far. But making her believe her life won't be the same without your presence, will take you much, much further. He must become a fixture, not a visitor. He has to make it so that the home doesn't feel the same if he's not around. He has to make it so that if he threatened to leave, she'd feel like her life would fall apart if he did. He must do his best to intertwine himself so much into your life that you couldn't imagine life without him.

"The Hobosexual okee-doke!"

Remember, he's skilled at what he does. Many of the mind games that he plays are very unique to the world of Hobosexuality. He'll use these various strategies to manipulate you, strategies that if you're not familiar with the lifestyle, you most likely won't be able to spot when he's using them. They are mind tricks that have you believing the choices you're making are of your own free will when it's actually his will that's guiding you. One mind trick that I've found to be his most powerful, is what I call the Hobosexual Okee-doke.

It's the main tactic, the signature move that any skilled Hobosexual will use. The Okee-doke is when a Hobosexual convinces his victim into believing that him moving in with her is actually her idea, not his. It's when the Hobosexual tricks his victim into inviting him to move into her home, all the while he's claiming that he doesn't think it's a good idea. The victim has been so brainwashed that she believes that it's her idea for him to give up all that he has going on in his life to be with her. It's allowing the victim to think that what's happening to her is her own doing. If he performs the Okee-doke correctly, she'll be begging him to move in with her. He'll pretend to be giving her good reasons why he shouldn't, putting her in a position of having to change his mind.

If the victim accepts that she's the driving force behind the conman moving in with her, then there's a responsibility for him that she also must accept. Any questionable behavior on his part becomes excusable after believing you've convinced him to give up his life to join yours. In fact, you knew he didn't really want to, therefore whatever happens after he's in there is on you. He wants to borrow your car, how can you deny him your car? He needs a few bucks to go shopping, you'll likely give up the cash so that he can shop. You knew he wasn't working before he came, so the nerve of you confronting him about not having a job? He didn't ask to be there in the first place, remember?

It would be difficult for a reasonable minded woman to throw a man out of her house when she is the same reasonable minded woman who begged the man to move in. She'd likely feel like a hypocrite if while the man lives with her, she doesn't allow that man to live the way he chooses to. And that's to do whatever he wants, eat whatever he wants, to come and go as he wants, to even treat her in a way that might not be to her liking. It's the Hobosexual Okee-doke.

"He'll cloud your mind with orgasms!"

To the Hobosexual, sex is used as a form of mind control. It's also used as a distraction. It's a way of getting a woman to look over there, while he does something over here. It's meant to keep your brain unable to focus. Sex most likely will mean one thing to you, while meaning something completely different to him. Whether sex is pleasurable for him is not a big concern for this conman, it's a bonus if it is, but it's just not needed. He's eyeballing something much more important, something much more valuable than any number of orgasms he could ever have with you. He's focused on maintaining a place to live.

Keeping you happy in bed is his way of getting you to drop your guard. Making sure you are sexually satisfied gets him in, it gets him by all the security measures that you may have in place to keep unsavory people from getting close to you. He'll use orgasms to manipulate you into opening more than your heart and legs, but also your home and purse. The more he knows you're enjoying the sex and wanting more of it, the more empowered he becomes. The trick is to get you to badly want him in your bed, so that he can satisfy his need to sleep in your bed. It's a trade-off he will be more than happy to make.

Good sex is what a Hobosexual uses to keep your mind trapped in a fog. And it's in that fog that you'll find yourself being taken advantage of. While dangling that tasty carrot of sex out in front of you, he will guide you blindly across some very questionable terrain that will benefit only him. It's like a pickpocket who intentionally bumps into you in order to distract you while he reaches in for your wallet. Or the used car salesman who blasts the car radio during your test drive, so you don't hear the weird noises coming from underneath the hood. Or the magician who directs your attention to his beautiful assistant as he pulls the rabbit out of his hat.

Keep in mind that sex is the Hobosexual's number one tool, and he's going to be very skilled at using it. You may find him better than most that you've ever slept with. This again is because his livelihood depends heavily on him being good at it. Most of them believe if they can just get into a woman's bedroom, having a place to stay just becomes academic after that. A Hobosexual is going to assume that a woman who is quick to allow a man to sleep in her bed, is a woman who is wanting or needing a man to share her home with. It may not be the reality for most women, but it's going to be a bet that the conman is willing to make.

Sub Three:

With Title Comes Power

Only a person in a position of power, can get away with wielding it!

"Attachment co-signing"

In an absolute crazy way, the Hobosexual's credibility as a person can become directly connected to, as well as measured by his victim's credibility. His victim becomes sort of a co-signer, a legitimizer. If the woman that he currently lives with is a person who deserves to be respected, then the Hobosexual's respect level can receive a great boost from just being associated with her. Like if the victim is a very educated and intelligent woman, the assumption will be that the Hobosexual is smart just by association. A man living with a very successful woman almost immediately is considered successful by those that meet him. The victim's success can make him appear successful. A broke and shiftless man who's living with a successful professional is not thought of as a broke and shiftless man. From the outside looking in, the assumption will be that he should be shown the same level of respect as she is shown. At least that will be the assumption by those who didn't know him prior to him living with her.

A stable victim can instantly make a Hobosexual appear stable, even to his loved ones. A Hobosexual's family and friends who knows the truth about how he lives, will usually have very little respect for him. In most cases, his loved ones really don't agree with the way he's chosen to live his life. Many Hobosexuals have used and abused those that care for him the same way they're trying to use and abuse you. He's likely caused so much trouble, that as much as they may love him, no one wants or trust having him around. He's most likely the black sheep of the family. But just like most of us, even the Hobosexual desires to be respected by those that he cares about. Unfortunately, this is something that he's unable to achieve on his own. But the right victim by his side could be just what the doctor ordered.

Many men who live this type of lifestyle also happen to be fathers. Some even end up having children with women that they have victimized. But just like how these men will disappear out of a woman's life and never to be seen again, these men are also known to do the same thing to the children that they produce. Most of them who are fathers, are also deadbeat dads. And just as his loved ones don't trust him as far as they can throw him, neither will his children. So what a Hobosexual will try to do is use that respectable woman that he is living with to build credibility with those same children that he previously neglected. He'll try to present himself as respectable, now that he has this respectable woman standing by his side. He'll attempt to use the credibility of his new woman to convince his kids that daddy is now credible.

I grew up with a guy, we'll call Cory, who lied more than anyone I ever knew. Since he was a kid, his ability to tell a tall tale was unmatched. It wasn't that Cory was necessarily a bad guy, most people liked him. It was just people also knew he had a very difficult time telling the truth about anything. I don't think that he meant to do anyone any harm, he was just someone who lying had become pathological. Because of this, he knew no one who spent a lot of time with him was never going to ever take his word for anything. Cory was not only a liar, but from my understanding, he also spent a lot of his early adult life living as a Hobosexual.

Unable to be truthful but wanting badly to be believed and trusted, Cory would turn to a technique that many Hobosexuals use to fix their lack of credibility problem. A technique that I call "attachment co-signing." It's when an untruthful person attaches themselves to someone who either because of their profession or their reputation, that person is considered unquestionably trustworthy and honest. Someone like Cory would use his association with a woman of high moral standards to bring credibility to his own claims and behavior.

One victim that Cory was involved with and tried to use attachment co-signing with was a woman name Tammy. Not only was she known for being a very trustworthy person, but for a dishonest Hobosexual like Cory, the icing on the cake was that Tammy was someone who also worked in law enforcement. And trust me, the first thing Cory did once he moved in with her was to make sure everyone knew what Tammy did for a living. In fact, he did this so much that more people knew that she was a cop than they knew what her name was. He did his best to make her name and occupation become synonymous with his own. Soon after moving in with her, Cory stopped using words like I, me, or mine. Instead, everything became "me and Tammy this" or "me and Tammy that."

She became Cory's unknowing co-signer. If Cory were to make a claim that he needed you to believe, the claim would always end with tags like: "ask Tammy" or "Tammy was there!" By adding these "Tammy tags", Cory believed her credibility would make his statements acceptable to the ears who heard them. Or that his stories deserved not to be questioned because of their connection to Tammy. Because of this, Cory wouldn't be caught out in public without her by his side. In her company, he felt folks showed him much more respect than they ever would if they met him alone. With Tammy, people who knew Cory well wouldn't just assume that everything that came out of his mouth was a lie. And this is what Cory was counting on, it was what he was hoping for. You see, for Cory, it wasn't actually necessary for him to change his dishonest ways, he just needed to change who stood beside him.

"Privileges of the babysitting stepdad"

Who needs a babysitter when there's an unemployed stepdad at home? A true Hobosexual will gladly contribute to a woman's life and household, as long as it doesn't require him to get a job. Like I spoke about earlier, he will do his best to become an asset to his victim, as long as it doesn't require him to contribute financially. And what better way to contribute, without having to un-ass the sofa and getting a job, than to be the live-in babysitter? For a homeless conman, meeting a woman with young children can be like hitting a jackpot. It's the perfect smoke screen, the perfect excuse for not working. Why should he try to find a job, when a man caring for your children is already doing you a huge favor. He's saving you a ton of money, he's allowing you to come and go as you please without being concerned with your children being properly supervised as you do.

In fact, some skilled conmen will place the blame for them not having a job directly on the lap of their victim if he is spending anytime watching that victim's kids. How can he maintain a job if he has to be constantly available to babysit? What better excuse can he have for sitting at home and watching television all day? Being the babysitting stepdad comes with perks that suit the Hobosexual just fine. It makes him immune to certain criticisms and ridicule. Under the stepdad umbrella, he can simply be who and what he wants to be without being concerned with anyone passing judgment on him.

And there's no better way to gain a woman's trust and admiration than to show love and care for her children. It's a direct pipeline into a woman's heart. Women will overlook the fact that her man does not contribute in any other way to the household, if she's able to depend on him to care for her children when she is unable to. Remember, the best position a Hobosexual can take in a victim's life is one in which the woman needs him, or one in which he serves a purpose. And for an unemployed man, there's no easier way of becoming an invaluable asset to a woman's household than to assist that woman with the care of her children.

It's very difficult to appreciate the hardship of being a single parent if you've never experienced it. I take my hat off to anyone who's able to raise children alone. This includes my mom, because even with my grandmothers help, I still don't know how she pulled it off. I can honestly see how a single mother who meets a man who shows genuine interest in helping her raise her children, could fall blindly head-over-hills for that man. She may be so appreciative for the help, she might be willing to do almost anything to show her gratitude, including overlooking some very questionable behavior. For the working single mom, having an unemployed boyfriend living in her home may be looked at as a blessing. Even if the boyfriend happens to be a Hobosexual masquerading as a blessing.

"Being your man insulates him"

Your loved ones will scrutinize some unemployed new guy who lives with you much differently than they would an unemployed boyfriend. Your "man" who you're caring for, who everyone accepts as the person they believe you're going to spend the rest of your life with, will be judged less harshly than some man that you're simply sleeping with. Most people that are close to a woman will be very reluctant to share their suspicions or distrust of an individual that the woman considers her future. Once a Hobosexual takes the position of significant other in a woman's life, it garners him a bit of protection.

The "your man" badge shields him from a lot of unnecessary attention that he just doesn't need, or unnecessary attention that could expose the game he's running. Being your man insulates him, it could keep his intentions from coming under question. As a victims' man, instead of someone she's just dating, keeps him from being looked at as a possible swindler or scammer, which he actually is. In most situations, holding down the title of her man makes the Hobosexual almost untouchable. It's the reason that they will do everything as quickly as they can, to gain that title in your life.

There's a difference between a guy you are dating driving your car, and your man driving your car. There's a difference between your man borrowing money from you, and a guy who you just met and moved into your home, borrowing money from you. Watch the difference in the response of your friends when you tell them that a guy you recently met is at home watching your kids, versus you telling them that your "man" is at home watching your kids. A person's title or position in your life can make all the difference in the world with what they're able to get away with in the eyes of people that care for you.

"Love means you're now responsible"

There's a lot of obligation that comes with announcing to someone that you love them. You basically can become responsible for their livelihood. It's why the Hobosexual will do almost anything to get you to feel that way about him. He knows if he can achieve that, you'll likely want to ensure that he is well cared for, that he has a roof over his head, food in his stomach, and even money in his pocket.

For most people, loving is the same as caring. A person getting you to love them can benefit them tremendously. Someone struggling tends to get more needed attention when he or she has people around that love them. It's very difficult to find a loved person suffering if the person who loves them is capable of ending their suffering. Most people will do almost anything for someone that they love. Being a person that someone loves places you in a position of always having help when or if you find that you need it. And that's a position that a Hobosexual strives to be in, and a position that he will most certainly take advantage of.

The Hobosexual needs his victim to at a minimum love him, or even better to be in-love with him. The closer he can get to in-love, the easier time he will have, the more he can take advantage of her. If it's just a friendly relationship, his position in the home cannot be considered a strong one, but instead, it's a weak and unstable position. It's very difficult for even a skilled Hobosexual to be successful at victimizing a woman if she doesn't have any feelings of love for him. How many women do you know who will give a man complete access to her home if she doesn't have any love for that man? The fact is, most aren't going to feel obligated to ensure that a person that they simply like is always comfortable and safe. Although you may be compelled to help them if you can, you just won't necessarily feel like it's your duty to do so. It's why in the mind of the Hobosexual, there's no bigger fool than a woman in love.

The conman is going to need his victim, in a very short period of time, to love and want to do for him the way a wife loves and wants to do for her husband. He needs to gain that same type of respect and adoration. With love guiding a woman's decision making, there's no limit to what a conman can get her to do. Where his behavior may be considered bad behavior through the eyes of someone who just likes him, that same behavior may be considered good behavior through the eyes of someone who loves him. It's the victim loving him that's gonna enable the Hobosexual to get his own key to the house, and his own key to the car. It's her loving him that will keep her from suspecting he's responsible for the cash that's missing from her purse. Love has a way of making a woman ignore the obvious lies that she catches her man telling. It's a fact that providing orgasms will get you far, but if he's also able to get the woman to love him on top of the orgasms, the sky's the limit to what he'll be able to get away with.

The Story of Bobby
"The Opportunist"

When I interviewed Bobby, he insisted that if I used his story in my project that I tell it exactly the way he told it to me, as close to word for word as possible. He was adamant about it. His concern was that I might change up his story for dramatic effect and make him look like a really bad guy. So, to honor his request, I simply recorded as Bobby told his story:

Man, I lived like that a few times in my life. Shit, when things go bad for you, what you going to do? The first time I did it I was living back in Milwaukee. I was working as a bartender in this hole-in-the-wall bar downtown. I had been in Milwaukee for about a year after I broke-up with my girlfriend and moved there from Texas. My buddy Cliff had just moved up there for a tech job he got, and he let me come visit him just to get away from everything that was going on with my ex. But after being there for just a few days, I decided to stay in Milwaukee for good. A lot of hot girls live there Bro', most guys just don't know it. Sure surprised the hell out of me.

I lived with Cliff for a couple months before I found a place of my own. I moved in with another bartender I worked with who was looking for a roommate. His name was Mike, and he was really cool, we used to hang out before I moved in with him, we were into a lot of the same stuff. We were both Texas boys, we clicked right away. We drank the same beer and liked the same type of women, and that goes really far, you know what I mean?! Neither one of us made a whole lot of money but we kept the lights on. All we did was work, drank and party. Man, we used to have a lot of fun.

Me, Mike and my other buddies used to crash parties all the time, we didn't care whose party it was. If the food and drinks were free, we were in there. You seen that movie Wedding Crashers? Well, that's the type of shit we was doing. I remember we crashed this one birthday party in this restaurant where this girl I knew was waiting tables. She was the one who told us about it. That was where I met Judy, it was actually her party. It was funny because we didn't know anyone there, so we had to act like we was coworkers of Judy's whenever anybody asked who we was. Boy did we feel dumb after finding out Judy was a veterinarian who worked alone in her office with just a damn secretary at the front desk. I mean, there goes the co-worker lie. People looked at us like we was crazy. But hell, we didn't care.

But Judy was real cool about it, because we came out and told her what we was doing there and she just laughed and told us we could stay. She didn't care. She was good looking too, I mean for her age and all. She was a lot older than me, damn near twenty years, I think. And I was about twenty-five at that time. Twenty-five or twenty-four. Me and Judy started hanging out, she didn't have a problem with the age difference. And one thing I learned from her was that older women don't mind paying when you're hanging out with them. I didn't even have to ask her to, she would just do it. It didn't matter what we did, the movies, dinner, whatever it was, Judy was cool with picking up the check. I don't know, maybe she knew my money was tight at the time. She made really good money. And it was only her, she didn't have any kids or family to take care of, so all her money was hers if you know what I mean. I don't think she had a man or anything like that when we met. Anyway, it wasn't like we was actually dating because I was definitely banging other chicks. I never asked her, and she never asked me what I was doing when I wasn't around her, so I just kept my mouth shut about it. I don't know if she was messing around with other guys, but I wouldn't have cared even if she was.

Yeah, we was sleeping with each other and all that, and we became really tight, but I only considered Judy a friend. She always would look out for me if I needed her. There was more than a few times when I was short on my end of the rent or something like that, and Judy always sprang into action. Even the times when I couldn't give it back, she never would ask me for it. I remember once when my car was in the shop and I couldn't get it out, Judy just came by the bar and dropped off the cash like it was nothing. I later gave that back to her because I really felt bad about her doing that one for me. She didn't want to take it, but I made her. My friends called her my sugar momma. I didn't really like that because like I said, I considered Judy my friend. But like with most chicks, the more we hung out, the more serious she wanted to get. And I definitely wasn't ready for anything serious. Hell, I was still trying to get over my ex, so you know I wasn't trying to settle down with Judy. She was cool and all, the sex was good, and we would have a few laughs every now and then, but I didn't want to be in a relationship with her, no way.

It didn't take her long to start doing weird shit like coming by the apartment unannounced, sometimes even when I wasn't there. Or stopping by the bar a lot after she got off work. Sometimes she'd try to hang around until I punched out. Problems really began for me when she started questioning me whenever she'd see another chick in my face. That's when I was like, nope, I gotta slow this train down before it gets out of control. I sat Judy down and told her what was up, I just wanted to be friends, nothing else. She had to give me some space or leave me the hell alone. I could tell her feelings were hurt, but it had to be said. After that, I wasn't seeing her around as much as I did before we had the talk. After a while, I wasn't seeing her around at all. And I was good with that because I was really done with the Judy thing anyway.

Then, I don't know why, but I started having some really bad luck, Bro'. I don't know who I pissed off upstairs, but the man above just wasn't happy with me for some reason. First, I lost my job, new management took over the bar and decided to bring in their own staff. They just showed up one day and told us we had two weeks. And just like that, I was out of work. Then my roommate decided he was tired of living in Milwaukee after we lost our jobs, so he packed up all his shit and moved back to Texas. We were barely able to make rent together so you know I couldn't do it alone, job or no job.

After Mike left, I spent weeks trying to find a new roommate, but couldn't find anybody. Even if I found somebody with a place and they were looking for a roommate, I had no job, and couldn't find a job no matter how hard I tried. The buddy I stayed with when I first got to Milwaukee was living with his girl now and she didn't like me, so I couldn't go over there. I damn sure wasn't gonna go back to Texas, back to that crap I left back there. Then that first eviction notice on the door put me into panic mode. I started calling everyone I knew, just to find a place to stay for a while but had no luck. Trust me, you learn really quick who your friends are when you need a place to sleep.

There was really only one person that I knew who I thought would let me come stay at their place, and that was Judy. The problem was, I hadn't seen or even talk to her a while, I mean months. Far as I know the lady could have gotten married or something like that. Plus, after that last conversation we had, I really didn't think she wanted to hear from me at all. But I had no choice at that point but to give Judy a shot. I had just four days before I was supposed to vacate the apartment. And in order for this Judy thing to work, before I asked her for help, I had to use those days to reconnect with her, and to get back on her good side.

Luckily, she was really excited to hear from me when I called. Gotta admit, I lied like hell. I told her I really missed her and invited her over to my place that same night. I didn't have time to play around. I had to first make her believe I really wanted to start spending time with her again. I wasn't even going to tell her about losing my job just yet. Because I knew she'd definitely start thinking something was up then. The better off I appeared to be doing, the better. So, she comes over and I put on a hell of a show.

I play like I was sorry I pushed her away, and that it wasn't until she was gone that I realized just how special she was and how much she meant to me. I think I even told her I loved her, but I'm not sure. I told her that I really hadn't seen anyone since her, and really had no desire to. Yeah, I laid it on thick. I didn't have time to lose, man, I was up against the clock. She saw that my roommate had moved out, but I lied and said that I had found someone who was going to be moving in a day or two so everything was cool. I told her that it was good that the new roommate was coming in, because if he wasn't I was going to have to give the apartment up. That was the main seed that I needed to plant in her head. She spent the night with me that night. And the next morning, when she told me she wanted to see me later that evening, I knew my plan was working like clockwork.

That next night we just repeated the previous night, but this time back at her place. I made sure Judy had a really good time too, sort of like how we used to, but even better. I remember turning everything up a notch, telling her things that I knew she wanted to hear, like how I was really at a point in my life where I thought I wanted to settle down with a really good woman like her. Things like how I never met anyone that made me feel the way she does. I laid it on thick that first night, but nothing compared to how I laid it on that second night. Hell, I think I even sucked on them toes that night. She was jelly in my hands. That next morning, we were both were exhausted, she didn't even go into work, we just laid around in her bed all day. But I had two more days before I had to be out of my apartment, so it was time for me to make my move.

I went home and waited for Judy to call me as she always would. When she did, I put on a performance that would have won me an Oscar. I put on like my world was coming to an end. I told Judy that the new roommate that I had found backed out of moving in and this meant I had to immediately give up the apartment. I told her that the bastard didn't even give me a reason why, he just left me hanging even though I told him if he didn't move in, I had to be out by the end of the month which was now just two days away. I pretended to be so upset, that I was honestly considering just packing my stuff up like Mike did and moving back to Texas. She didn't want to hear me talking like that. She basically demanded I get my stuff and come stay with her. I first played like that was out of the question. And the more I resisted, the more she insisted. So finally, after she practically begged and begged, I agreed to do it. I agreed to move in with her only until I find another place of my own.

Let me say this, and make sure you put this in the book. I honestly went into staying with Judy just long enough for me to find another job and another situation I could afford. I was thinking it would only take me a few weeks tops. But damn if I didn't end up staying with that woman for over a year. And to be honest, the longer I was there, the more I realize why I didn't want to be in a relationship with her in the first place. Judy was a goddamn pain in the ass. But I couldn't complain, I had to keep my mouth shut, she was hooking me up and wasn't asking me for nothing. Even when I finally told her about my job situation, she didn't care about that either.

Bro', the woman was really taking care of me. I don't know if you've seen that old film Sunset Boulevard, well, Judy was starting to make me feel like that guy in that movie. She was always buying me stuff. She even took care of my cell phone, kept plenty of food and my favorite beer in the fridge. To tell you the truth, after I was there a few months, I just stopped looking for a job all together. She didn't have a problem with me not working so why get one? She was giving me money any time I needed it, so it wasn't like I needed the cash. All I had to do is keep her believing I was gonna be there for good and I wasn't gonna need for nothing. She started giving me a hard time for hanging out with my friends, but whenever she'd complain about something too much, I'd just threaten to move out and she'd shut up.

Me: So, when did everything change?

Like I said, I was there for about a year. And I was just tired of Judy. I only was having sex with her to keep her off my back. But then she started nagging me about everything, like we were married or some shit. What you doing? Where you going, and who's gonna be there? I just couldn't take it anymore. it got to the point where I didn't care how good I had it, I just couldn't hack it. I took a bartending job, and I did that just to get out of the house and away from her. I started sleeping with chicks that I would meet at work. Of course, Judy didn't know about it. At least I don't think she did. Things really changed though when I started hanging out with Beth, a woman who came through the bar one night with a couple of her friends. She was the complete opposite of Judy. She was more like me, she liked to party and have fun. Judy was boring, Bro'. But what else you gonna expect from a woman who's close to fifty? Beth was the same age as me, so we had more in common. I really started to like Beth. And I know she was liking me too because she knew all about Judy and didn't seem to care. And when I told her how much I hated living with Judy, Beth just told me to come live with her, and that's what I did. I waited for Judy to go to work one day and packed my stuff up and left. I never talked to her again.

CHAPTER FOUR

Just How Dangerous Are They?

Sub One:

Many Are Criminals

A liar is a thief's close cousin. And often times when you're dealing with one, you're dealing with the other.

"Some may rob you blind"

There's a number of Hobosexuals that just don't come into your life and home in search of a place to sleep, many are in search of things to steal, with money being the number one item on the list; followed by any other thing of value that you may have such as jewelry, electronics, all the way up to the car that you drive. If a thieving Hobosexual believe he can make money off of it, your property will be in jeopardy the moment he makes his way into your home. He'll clean you out if given the chance to do so. And by allowing the wrong one in, it will be all the chance he needs.

A person who doesn't have a job is going to have a need for cash, it's just that simple. For most Hobosexuals, after a soft pillow and maybe some food, money is going to be the next thing he's going to be looking for. From the loose change you keep in a coffee cup in the kitchen, or a few bills out of your purse when you're not looking, to thousands of dollars he'll withdraw from your bank account. Any and all money that you have may be at risk. If he has no source of income coming in, you and everything that you have of value becomes his source of income.

I know of a woman who discovered that the man she had moved into her home was a thief only after money and property around the house began to disappear. It started out small, just a few bucks that would occasionally come up missing around the house. But it wasn't until she began noticing money gone from her bank account that she realized who and what she had living with her. Her new man who had been with her for just a month or so, was waiting until she was asleep, taking her bank debit card and withdrawing cash a little at a time from ATM machines. And if she hadn't figured it out when she did, there was no doubt in her mind that he would have continued doing it as long as he could get away with it.

Unfortunately, many victims don't discover what they're dealing with until it's too late. Some women are completely wiped out before realizing there's a thief living in the house. Instead of a few bucks missing, many women find their accounts completely emptied out. It's not just a few bucks from an ATM, for some it's thousands of dollars that's gone before realizing that their new man is the culprit.

For the average Hobosexual, the number one goal is to find a warm bed or couch to sleep on, it's not to steal your money. But unfortunately, many end up doing just that. Even for some that don't go into the situation with stealing on their agenda, they end up doing so anyway out of necessity. Chances are he's not working, and if for some reason you're not giving him any cash, where is he gonna get money from? He's gonna have to get it from somewhere. And if he's living with you, who's money is closer to him than yours? A Hobosexual is going to consider what you have partially his anyway, so why not treat himself every now and then to the goodies?!

"Many are wanted men"

There has been accounts of women moving a new man into their home and later finding out that the men were wanted by the law for committing various types of crimes. Everything from theft to robbery, to assault up to murder. Many of them not only may be using your home as a place to rest their heads, but it may turn out that your home is also being used as a place to hide. You will not be able to simply look at these men and be able to tell that they are fugitives, so if you think that you're safe because you believe you would recognize a criminal when you see one, you better think again. He could have just finished a cross-country crime spree just days prior, and still look like a choir boy the day that you meet him.

One victim found out the hard way that her new man was wanted, when a heavily armed police swat team kicked in her front door in the middle of the night. Her Hobosexual was on the run for committing multiple armed bank robberies. Another woman in Texas met a guy online, allowed him to move in with her soon after meeting him, only to be later charged with harboring a fugitive from justice because he was wanted for murder in Florida. Despite what you see in movies, most criminals do not look like criminals. If they did, they would not be able to commit as many crimes as they do.

Then there's the women who have moved men into their homes, only to later find out that they are not single without children the way the men claimed, but instead they are still legally married and fathers to many children. To make the deception worse, the men had not only abandoned their families, but they were wanted for not paying court ordered child support. The men were simply looking for a place to hide out. And what better place to hide out than in the home of a woman that not only doesn't really know the man, but the home of a woman that those who do know him, don't know her.

The question you must ask yourself is do you really know who you are allowing into your home, or who you are having sex with? Do you really know this person who you are bringing around your children and loved ones? Most women cannot honestly answer yes to these questions because many fail to check the backgrounds of men that they begin seeing. The fact of the matter is, unless you properly vet a man that you meet, the only thing you will know about the man is what he chooses to tell you, what he wants you to believe.

If you think about it, the Hobosexual lifestyle would work perfectly for someone who is on the run. Like the Hobosexual, the fugitive from justice is gonna basically be homeless, and in need of a place to stay where whoever he lives with, does not know him very well. Someone on the run needs to be somewhere anyone who might know him, or who's on the lookout for him, would not have a clue that he is there. Also, the only thing that a man on the run may have to offer you is conversation and a good time in the sack. Sounds awfully familiar, doesn't it?

"The new online predator"

Online dating is a great place for a lonely person to find love, and a wonderful place for a social predator to find a place to sleep. It can be a fantastic way for a woman who may be desperately in need of affection and attention, to unknowingly match herself up with a man who is desperately in need of a roof over his head. Online dating sites and social media pages are places where both types of people can thrive and find success. It is a great place for victim to encounter victimizer, predator to find prey.

Commonly used dating site self-advertisements such as "Professional woman seeking professional man for long term relationship" would be something that most Hobosexuals wouldn't be able to resist responding to. "Lonely woman seeking companionship", would have a Hobosexual drooling at the mouth. To him, you might as well be wearing an "I'm-looking-to-be-taken-advantage-of" t-shirt. Searching for love over the internet can and will expose you to all type of scammers, especially a conman who is on the lookout for women searching for someone to cuddle up with at night.

There are even stories of women who after discovering the men that they had living with them were Hobosexuals, the women also discovered evidence that the men had used the women's own computers to meet other victims on online dating sites. The internet has given predators the ability to reach out and lure victims all from the comfort of a laptop or cellphone. This means he can connect with you from anywhere at any time. This also gives him the ability to pretend to be whoever he wants to be. Like any other type of online scammer, the internet allows him to create and customize the perfect persona that he believes a potential victim will be attracted to. And for a man with no money, the internet also allows him to win a woman over without spending a dime.

Dating and social media sites now give the Hobosexual the ability to not only find his next victim, but it gives him the ability to target the exact area where he'd like to live. Where before he would have to be more of an opportunist when hunting, the internet gives him the ability to be much more proactive and intentional in his approach. Instead of having to get to know a woman in order to find out if she is someone who would make a good target, women today freely and openly share all the info a conman needs to know. Things like, "Recently divorced and ready to mingle," "Single, no kids, no drama", "Lonely heart looking for love", and one of my favorites and I'm sure also a favorite of a social scam artist, "God fearing woman looking for long-term relationship." Posts like these on dating sites are like an emergency homing beacon flashing in the dark to social predators. And it can give him all the info that he needs to customize the perfect bait to dangle out in front of you.

How you interact with people online, as well as what you share online, can also tell a lot about you. How friendly are you with strange men, how do you respond to them when they openly hit on you? Are you very flirty, are you looking for attention? Do you openly share your feelings on sex?

Is it obvious that your goal is to become popular? Are you posting photos of yourself scantily dressed? Do you ever show photos of you with children? Are most of the photos that you post show you spending money, shopping, and traveling? These are all things that a skilled Hobosexual who is considering targeting you is going to be paying attention to. So be very careful with your online footprint.

"What he knows makes him a threat"

Something that you must keep in mind when you're trying to separate yourself from a Hobosexual, before you throw him out onto the street, there's nothing about you that he does not know. It's part of his agenda, to make himself aware of everything about a victim that he is living with. And this fact makes kicking him out, which you have no choice but to do, very dangerous. Because you're not only kicking a man out of your life, but you're also kicking a man out who knows more about you than you ever want to imagine. And now this lying scoundrel has all the information about you that he could ever need to turn your entire life upside down if he were inclined to do so.

A conman living in your home has access to your life in ways that no one else could ever gain. The more he knows about you, the better he can take advantage of you. In the world of Hobosexuality, information is king. He has to know your habits, your likes and dislikes, your urges, and desires. He must familiarize himself with your fears and pet-peeves, as much as your turn-ons. He has to know what makes you click. He needs to know what your goals are, or what if any secret fantasies you may have. Therefore, he's going to need to know where your personal diary or journals are kept. And the answer to the question you're now asking yourself is yes, if he found them, he has read your diary and journals from cover to cover.

He's gonna know what places you frequent the most, the restaurants where you like to eat, the stores where you like to shop. He's gonna know where you bank, where your doctor or dentist office is located. He's gonna familiarize himself with where your family and friends live. Any place you need to go, or like to go, he's gonna know where these places are. He's gonna know where your children attend school, their favorite places to play and hang out. He's gonna have all this knowledge, and this is a man you're possibly about to make an enemy of yours by kicking him out of your house.

More importantly, he's going to know where you keep your treasures, where you like to hide the good stuff. A Hobosexual living with you is going to search your home every chance he gets until he locates anything that's of any value. And don't think for a second that your ability to hide your valuables is better than his ability to find them, because it's not. If something that you have is worth anything to him, he's gonna know where you keep it. So, you must always remember, an unpredictable person that knows everything about you can be an extremely dangerous person to now be turning against you.

Sub Two:

Mentally And Physically Abusive

Most people who hurt others are usually people who are hurting themselves. And show me a person with no place to call home, and I'll show you a person who is in a lot of pain.

"Murder by a different name"

The following story happens hundreds of times a year throughout the globe. A woman meets a man on an online dating app, and soon after invites the man to visit her at her home. The two hit it off so well after just one visit, that the man moves in with her with just the clothes on his back. Then tragically, the woman ends up dead, and the man is later convicted for her murder. Now where the woman lived, the headline on the local news was, "Another online date goes bad." When in my opinion, the headline could have easily been, "A Hobosexual kills his victim soon after moving in." Both headlines could have been an accurate depiction of the event. But because the term Hobosexual has not made it into the vocabulary of most people, I believe there are actually many murders perpetrated by Hobosexuals every year that are not reported as murders by Hobosexuals. The term Hobosexual just wasn't, at least at the time that I was penning this project, a very popular term. But I believe if it had been, the way some murders are reported would be drastically different.

I'm sure you've all heard about someone being killed by a person who they knew only for a very short period of time before allowing them to move into their home. I'm not saying that all these were crimes committed by a Hobosexual, But I am suggesting that we can't rule out that many of them weren't. If you were to look into the case files of many of these crimes, you'll find that the description of the relationship between the victim and perpetrator, meets the criteria of a Hobosexual/ victim relationship. I believe if the term Hobosexual was, in the eye of the law, an accepted description of a person's behavior, many of these situations would have been classified as Hobosexual Homicides. If I were asked to guess, I'd say that Hobosexuals are responsible for a number of murders each year. The consensus definition of a Hobosexual is a person who enters a sexual relationship merely to have a place to stay. And I'm quite sure that many men who kill the women who allow them into their homes, those men were badly in need of a place to stay.

I'm willing to wager that many horrific crimes committed by Hobosexuals have been written off simply as cases of domestic violence. Two people living together, one kills the other, how else would most agencies classify the crime? It's the easy way out, even if the people reporting it isn't looking for the easy way out. But I personally believe, if you were to dig deeper into many of these cases of live-in boyfriend killing girlfriend in her home, you'll find plenty of evidence of the crime being one committed by a social conman.

"They can become stalkers"

Like I said before, most Hobosexuals when their victim catches on to the con they're running, will usually just leave, to never be seen again. Normally the worst that will happen is that the victim will notice a few of her valuables gone along with him. But there are the occasional Hobosexual who for whatever reason or another decides that they don't want to let you go. Every now and then you hear about one who although he leaves when you tell him to leave, he doesn't actually leave you alone. He begins stalking you.

For many of them, if they stay with you long enough, you not only become their only means of support, but you also become their only means of survival. Despite the fact that they have been conning and misleading you, some become delusional into believing that you really are their significant other. They have convinced themselves that the two of you are a couple. And as a couple, your home and everything in it, is his just as much as it is yours. Again, they have become delusional. And that delusion can cause them to become very dangerous.

The conman may not want to give you and your home up without a fight, he may linger around in an attempt to convince you to give him another chance. He may want to plead his case, or he may want an opportunity to explain himself and his behavior. Even if you stand by your decision to put him out, he may come back in an attempt to change your mind. He may return again, and again, and again, and again. If he can't convince you to give him another chance at your home, he may start showing up at your workplace and try to convince you. If that don't work, he may try you at your gym, or the grocery store where you're known to shop. Maybe the salon where you get your hair done, or the cleaners where you drop off your laundry. He could've been living with you for months, so he knows where to find you if he wants to find you. And if he is determined to get back into your good graces, he may start popping up where you would least expect him.

To be a Hobosexual, one has to always believe he's the smartest person in the room. Therefore, despite his victim exposing him as a conman, he may still be arrogant enough to believe he can manipulate his victim if he can only get the opportunity to speak with her again. And if he's convinced that he can somehow get his victim to change her mind about allowing him to stay, he'll do everything in his power to get a moment of her time to try to do just that. And like gum stuck on the bottom of a shoe, it may take a victim a bit of work to rid herself of a man who doesn't want to leave her alone. A man who refuses to take no for an answer, could easily become a danger to you. The Webster Dictionary definition of a stalker is:

"A person who pursues someone obsessively and or aggressively to the point of harassment."

Depending on how dependent on you that the Hobosexual may have come to be, he may not leave your life so quietly. In fact, he may choose to not leave without a fight, even as you're insisting that he must go. Regardless of if he's lived with you for only a few weeks or for a few years, in a delusional conman's mind, it's not just your home anymore, it's the home the two of you had been sharing. It's the home where the two of you have been building a life together, despite if it was under very false pretenses. He may not want to give you up without a fight.

It's similar to if you were on a boat out in the ocean and you came across a person who's drowning. You threw them a lifeline, but regardless of how hard you try, you cannot pull them out of the water, so you decided to stop trying to save him. Well, just because you decide to let go of your end of the lifeline, doesn't mean that they're gonna let go of theirs. They may continue to grip tightly to that lifeline as if they were to let go, they're gonna lose their life. Just the way the Hobosexual may feel about the lifeline of living with you that you've tossed him some time back. Although you decide to give up, he may not be so ready to drown. He may do any and everything to stay afloat.

A person refusing to leave your life can easily become dangerous, you should not be dealing with this situation alone. Bring your problem to the attention of your friends and family, make sure everyone knows that he is no longer wanted in your home so that they can be on alert for any foolishness. There's no telling what a desperate man will do, he may fight you tooth and nail. And if he can't convince you to change your mind and allow him to stay, he may decide to punish you for asking him to leave.

"From lover to witness"

One of the worst places you can find yourself, is standing between a disturbed individual, and a possible prison sentence. Some people will do anything to avoid being incarcerated, including getting rid of any potential witnesses that are willing and able to help place them there. In that one instance when you confront a Hobosexual and threaten to call the cops, you can go from being his lover and caregiver, to someone that can point him out to a judge. And it's then that you can become someone that he can't allow to live. I realize this scenario is very uncommon and very rare, unfortunately it's still a possible scenario that you need to be fully aware of, especially if you're dealing with an individual who is unstable.

When you are throwing a man out of your home, you are literally pulling his life as he knows it right from underneath his feet. Your home had become his home, you may have even fed and clothed him, provided him with cash, he may have had access to your car whenever he needed it. And just like that, you take all that away, he's now on the street with nothing and no place to go. To make matters even worse for him, he knows if you choose to, you can make his life much more difficult than you already have.

Although you may not have any intention on making it worse, but that's not the issue for him. The issue is you simply having the ability to do so if you choose. And now that he knows that you consider him an adversary, he may not be able to live comfortably with you possessing that type of power over his life.

Being the only thing standing between a Hobosexual moving on with his life or being arrested, may not be a position you want to find yourself in. Women have come up missing for a hell of a lot less. A person who feels he's finally gained some credibility in his life may kill just to keep from being outed as a conman. The idea of you exposing what he really is to the world may not be something that he feels he can allow to happen. Especially if he believes you plan to out him to your friends and family, whom he now considers his friends and family. The idea of you turning those people against him may be enough to make him snap.

I must reiterate, most Hobosexuals are not dangerous people. The vast majority of these men are simply looking for a place to sleep, not to bring you any harm. But like with anything else in the world, there's always gonna be exceptions to the rule, the chance of you grabbing the one rotten apple from the basket. And chances are you won't know you have a rotten one until you take a bite. You likely won't know that you're dealing with a crazy man who has the ability to bring you physical harm, until he brings you physical harm. When he felt he had you under his control, there was no reason for him to reveal that he was unstable. But now that you have stripped him of his power and taken back all the comforts and support that you were providing him, all bets are off.

"Dr Jekyll and Mr. Hyde"

Many Hobosexuals can be gentle and harmless one moment and become psycho-violent the next. It could happen in the blink of an eye. A Hobosexual can have dangerous personality disorders just like anyone else that you may meet. They're no different. Many of them are unable to lead normal lives because of this issue. It's the reason why some can only live as Hobosexuals in the first place. Some are timebombs just waiting to explode. Move the wrong one into your home, and you may discover this the hard way.

Dr Jekyll & Mr. Hyde told the story of a normally nice, mild-mannered scientist who created a potion that when he drunk it, the potion transformed him into his alter ego which was a crazy homicidal maniac. But if you're dealing with a mentally unstable conman, it's gonna be more likely that you're faced with a person who is really a crazy homicidal maniac, who's alter ego is a gentle mild-mannered guy. Being who he actually is, a crazy maniac, won't get him a place to sleep. Being the crazy person that he truly is most likely won't motivate you to fall in love with him. You're not gonna let a Mr. Hyde drive your car or watch your kids while you're working. He's going to have to create a Dr. Jekyll to present to you in order to win you over. No reasonable person is going to move a crazy person into their home unless they don't know him to be crazy. And unfortunately, you may not learn someone is crazy until they exhibit crazy behavior. That person that you've just allowed to move into your home very well may appear sane, until he isn't. It's why you must really get to know someone before allowing them access to your personal space. Let the wrong one get close to you and you could be dealing with someone who, despite appearing to be very mild mannered, is actually very dangerous.

Unlike Jekyll and Hyde, your new guy won't need a potion to cause him to transform. Anything might trigger the change. If he's truly unstable, something simple or relatively innocent could do the trick. The raising of your voice, feeding him the wrong meal, denying him sex or attention, not keeping your home neat and clean. Any behavior that you may consider normal behavior could actually do it. He could even flip at that first sign that he doesn't have complete control over you. The first time that you deny him of something may send him over the deep end. There are countless cases of women experiencing men who they just recently began dating, suddenly snapping and behaving very violently. It's not as uncommon as you may think.

An unstable person living off his wit can turn dangerous when or if the pressure of trying to keep up his fake persona becomes a bit too much for him. They're basically living a lie to keep a roof over their head. Everything that they do, everything that they say, has to be calculated and carefully planned out in order to keep from being exposed as a phony. Imagine the mental strain that one must endure in order to wake up every morning knowing that with just one slip of the tongue, life as you know it could be over. And you must keep in mind that a man who you're taking care of and having fun with can become a completely different person the moment he becomes a man you are throwing out of your home. If he has a Hyde side, that's the moment I'd bet that you're going to be introduced to it. A secretly unstable conman may not handle the idea of losing his meal ticket very well. Becoming homeless may not be a pill that he can again swallow after having it so good living with you. You really don't know this man, so you really don't know if at a moment like that, he won't become an out of control crazed mad scientist. The moment you do find out he suffers from a Jekyll and Hyde complex, could be the last moment you find out anything ever again.

Sub Three:

Destruction In Their Wake

You gotta understand how much damage they can cause, in order for you to appreciate the importance of protecting yourself.

"Danger, the transmitted kind"

A man who is vine swinging from victim to victim, from bed to bed, is bound to be carrying a social disease or two along with him. It's inevitable. Herpes, gonorrhea, syphilis, crabs, and other diseases are going to be prevalent amongst men who make a living using their bodies as currency. Socially transmitted diseases are always a huge risk for anyone who has unprotected sex with folks that they barely know. But you greatly increase your chances when dealing with a Hobosexual. He may be using sex with you to crash in your bed this week, but who was he sleeping with last week to maintain a place to sleep? Or the week before that, and the week before that?

It is quite common for a Hobosexual to be gaming more than a couple of victims at one time. Depending on the level of skill and experience that he has, sometimes the number can be higher than a couple. Either way, when living with this type of social conman, your bed becomes one giant petri dish. Although you may see him walk in with just his overnight bag, the problem is what he is carrying into your home that you can't see. Although you may not hear about it, many women actually die from the diseases that they contract from these temporary live-in situations. The biggest culprit, AIDS. Here's some facts that I found from 2022, the year this book was written:

... By 2022, there were approximately 1.4 million people living with HIV in the US. 1 in 7 of these people didn't even know they suffered from the virus.

... Over 700,000 people are known to have died from AIDS in the US alone.

... It was believed that only 66% of the people living with HIV were receiving medical treatment. And despite the great medical advances that have been made in the treatment of HIV and AIDS, people are still dying of it every day.

For the Hobosexual, revealing that he's infected with some social disease will certainly hinder his ability to keep his position in your home, food in his stomach, and money in his pocket. If it comes down to a choice between remaining homeless or telling someone he's carrying a sexually transmitted disease, he's most likely gonna keep his mouth shut. He just can't take the risk of his victim discovering he's infected with anything when his number one way of manipulating her is with sex. A Hobosexual has to remain quiet about any diseases that he's possibly carrying. For him, he really has no choice. When you live as a conman, honesty is not your friend, lying and withholding information is.

The careless and irresponsible way that these men run their game is a major cause of the way sexual diseases are spread throughout communities all over the world. For most of them, risking infecting their caregivers is a risk that they are willing to take. Whether it's knowingly or unknowingly infecting his victim, a Hobosexual can be one of the most dangerous people that you could choose to bring into your home. Again, it's not the things that he's bringing along with him that you're able to see that you need to be concerned about, it's the things that you can't see that should concern you.

"Financial ruin"

In most cases, victims of Hobosexuals will only be injured emotionally. Despite that, there are the occasions where victims are left in absolute dire straits financially. Many are left in such bad shape, that they actually never recover from it. Some have lost their homes, their savings and or their credit is extremely damaged. You name a way a person's life can be completely destroyed monetarily, and some skilled Hobosexual has left some poor woman suffering that way. Getting mixed up with the wrong conman can have devastating financial repercussions. He can leave you without a cent to your name, not even enough for a cup of coffee. A conman who targets a woman for her bed as well as her money may go into the situation with the intent to completely clean her out.

Once inside your home, the wrong Hobosexual will quickly begin looking for ways to enrich himself. A man who has lived with you even for a short period of time may have discovered where you keep your check book. He writes one out to himself for cash, and as he disappears, so does all the money from your checking account. If not your check book, he grabs your debit card. You know, the card you let him use every now and then to buy things for the house. You considered him your man, so why wouldn't he have the security pin code for the card? And after cleaning you out, all you can do is be mad at yourself for allowing him access to your finances the way you did.

Maybe it won't be your money that he steals, maybe he'll destroy your credit by making purchases in your name. Because you've given him full access to your home, that means he's had full access to everything inside it. And that unfortunately means anything with your personal information on it. We're talking about your birth certificate and social security card, your driver's license and passport. Your tax documents, as well as documents for your business if you have one. Any and everything that a criminal needs to steal your identity and start a line of credit in your name for himself. He's seen your bank information, investment documentation, even all the stuff pertaining to the mortgage to your home. Without intentionally doing so, you've given him access to any and everything that he could possibly need to destroy your life with just a few pecks at a computer's keyboard.

Some women are left financially ruined, not by the Hobosexual stealing from them, but rather by the conman convincing them to invest in his crazy get rich quick schemes. Like the aspiring music producer who doesn't have the money to finance building his own studio, so he manipulates his victim into investing thousands to make that happen. And his victim, who has grown to love him and want to keep her man happy, spends every dime to her name to see that he gets what he wants.

He'll have her believing that once he hits it big, she's also gonna hit it big. He'll convince her that she's not investing money in him, but rather she's investing money into their future together. Instead of it being "his" business venture, it's "their" business venture. And after investing her life savings, she'll quickly discover that she had a better chance at hitting it big, if only she placed all that money on a one-legged turtle in a rabbit race. I speculate that many women foolishly believe that way of keeping a man somewhat obligated to them, is to finance a man's hopes and dreams. This is surely a foolish way of thinking, and a way of thinking that has left countless women broke and broken hearted.

You may be surprised to find that the vehicles of many of the men that you meet, are actually in the names of the women that they either are living with or have lived with in the past. Better yet, women that they victimized in the past. Some of these men are driving cars that are not only in someone else's name, they are driving cars that they most certainly can't afford. And when these men get to the point where the car becomes too much of a financial burden, they'll just let the bank repossess it, badly damaging the woman's credit. Or he'll simply return the car to the woman, forcing her to deal with payments that are months and months behind, on a car that she never really wanted in the first place. Now she's forced to keep the car and maintain the payments just to keep her credit from being destroyed. Hobosexuals have done this type of thing with home loans, business loans, as well as large personal loans. They'll get a victim who they are living with to take out a loan for them, promising the victim that they will pay the loan back, only to later disappear leaving the victim holding the bag.

Hobosexuals are not going to rob you wearing a ski mask and holding a gun, they're going to be armed with a bouquet of roses in one hand, and a hard penis in the other. It doesn't matter if you're independently wealthy, or living on public assistance and barely making it, a money hungry social predator will target you if he thinks he can enrich himself. And he won't mind destroying your life, and leaving you broke in the process.

"Scorched earth"

You must remember, when you throw a man who you've been allowing to live with you out of your house, you're throwing him out of "his" house. As crazy as it may sound, in his mind you're throwing him out of the home that belongs to the both of you. I know it's hard to believe he could think that way, but many do and will. You've essentially taken his world away from him. Because of this, the Hobosexual may become bitter, and may seek to burn down that same world that he's bitter about losing.

The military strategy of scorched earth is a policy in which a departing army destroys any and everything in an area it occupies that can be used by an enemy after that army leaves. The departing army may completely render unusable any equipment, shelter, vehicles, or food source. A departing army may do this as a strategy in war, while a Hobosexual will possibly be doing this out of spite or anger. He could also do this seeking vengeance. He may take his anger out on things that you care about. Anything associated with you may become a target, anything that he may believe will bring you pain.

There are some people, who if forced to cross a bridge that they don't want to cross, will burn that bridge down behind them. There are folks that for whatever reason you force them out of your life, will feel compelled to hurt you after you do so. Many delusional men trick themselves into believing that if they burn down the bridge into your life after they've crossed over it, it's a way of keeping another man from crossing back over it to take their place. There's no way he is going to allow another man to enjoy the life he has been enjoying the last few months. He may confuse the time he's spent conning you with time he's spent investing in you. And rarely does someone want to just give up anything that they've heavily invested in.

Some Hobosexuals are mentally unstable, so imagine what can happen to an unstable mind when that mind starts wanting vengeance. You can easily find yourself dealing with a crazy person who is now crazy and angry. It's very easy for crazy and angry to morph into vengeful. It's very easy for crazy, angry, and vengeful to morph into destructive. And a destructive man who's lived with you even for a short period of time knows what to damage on his way out the door that will cause you the most pain.

A recently evicted and now spiteful Hobosexual may show up at your job in an attempt to get back at you. Women have come out to find obscene words written on their cars, bricks thrown through their windshields, or their tires slashed. Some pissed-off conmen have even taken to contacting a woman's place of business to spread false rumors about them. Many women have had to take leave of absences, while others have actually been fired from their jobs because of this type of foolishness. And getting you fired may be just the payback he needs for you throwing him out of the house.

A Hobosexual may feel he was doing you a favor by living with you. As far as he's concerned, you should be grateful that you had the privilege of sleeping with him. This type of arrogance may cause him to be extremely insulted that you've asked him to leave, even if you kicked him out because you discovered he's a lying and manipulative social predator. But like I always say, if you don't really know someone well, you can't predict how they are going to act once the two of you cross swords. You're basically dealing with a scorned stranger that you just made homeless. You just turned a man who once was your trusted lover, into a stranger who may now hate your guts.

"Divide and conquer"

One technique the Hobosexual may use to gain control over your life is to isolate you, separating you from those in your life who care. He'll do this if he finds that your family and friends could interfere with the influence that he's trying to have over you. If the people around you can get in his way, he will attempt to remove them from your life. He may attempt to do this by making you believe you can't trust them, that they don't have you best interest in mind, at least not the way that he does. Whatever it takes to make you sour toward them, he's going to do it if he feels that getting rid of them makes his position in your life stronger.

He'll try to get you to believe that the same people who have always been there for you actually have ulterior motives for being in your life. Or that they could be the reason that your life isn't prospering. Although he's doing everything that he can possibly do to take advantage of you, he'll try to convince you that it's your loved ones that you have to be worried about, not him. He'll be relying on your desire for him in your life to influence you to trust his view of your loved ones over your own. And unfortunately, many women will alienate the folks who truly care about them, all because they have a manipulative conman whispering in their ear.

The ideal situation for a Hobosexual would be to win over the hearts and minds of your family and friends, instead of turning you against them. Making your loved ones his allies can make his position in your life even stronger. But if he can't win them over, he may resort to creating a wedge between you and them. They can't get in the way if they aren't around. It's just not to his advantage to have someone in your life with more influence over you than he has. Anyone who cares about you may be a threat to him, especially if they begin to question his character or position in your life. Your family and friends simply can become collateral damage. It won't matter if it's your parents, your children, your siblings or best friend. The longer he stays with you, the more loved ones you may lose. If he lives with you too long, you may find yourself without a friend in the world.

There was a single mom who lived alone with her two teenaged boys. The woman was in her late forties, divorced and working as a cashier at a local grocery store. Her boys never really gave their mom any trouble and were considered very well-behaved and respectable kids as far as the neighborhood was concerned. The small family shared a very tight bond. Then she met a new man. And after only a few weeks of knowing him, the woman allowed him to move in with her and the boys. Needless to say, her sons, as well as the woman's friends and family, were all against it.

Then everything seemed to change overnight. Because unbeknownst to her at the time, the man was a conman down on his luck, and badly in need of a place to stay. Almost immediately after he unpacked, the new man and the boys began bumping heads. First of all, the boys didn't like him, and they had every reason not to. They were able to see things that their mother, who was too head-over-hills in love, could not see. Despite their young ages, they recognized a user when they saw one. He didn't have a job. They watched as he would lounge around on the sofa watching television all day, while their mom was away hard at work. After a while, they saw their mom begin to struggle financially because of the additional grown mouth to feed. The new man didn't have a car of his own, and her sons hated the way he would disappear with their mother's car, leaving the family with no transportation for days at a time. The boys weren't blinded by a desperate desire to not be alone the way mom was. Therefore, they were able to see through his bullshit, and they just didn't like what they saw.

The woman's sons began to voice their feelings about the situation to their mom, as well as to their relatives. This caused a lot of tension and friction in the house. Some of the woman's relatives started questioning her about their concerns regarding the new guy, but she would always defend him, and often times refuse to discuss it. The confrontations between her sons and the boyfriend began to occur more frequently, with some of them nearly turning violent, and mom having to play referee. The battles would go on for months. And when the new boyfriend began to believe the woman's children were becoming an obstacle that he may not be able to overcome, he chose to do something about it. It was either going to be him or her sons. Unfortunately, the man at that point had such a grip on their mother, that the boys never stood a chance. They were sent to live with Grandma, and the boyfriend had the mom as well as the home all to himself.

The Story of Tim
"The Thief"

A few years ago, I heard about a guy in Atlanta, we'll call him Tim, who one day met a very attractive and much younger man while working out at his local gym. Tim was in his late forties, the owner of a popular restaurant who at the time, lived alone despite being in a ten-year relationship with his then boyfriend. The young man was new to the gym and told Tim he was a personal trainer who was open to helping him with his workouts if he ever needed him to. Like most of the other folks at the gym, Tim assumed the young man's claim of being a trainer was true because he was described to have had the body of someone who took his diet and working out very seriously.

The young man becomes a staple at the gym, Tim begins seeing him there every time he would go. And when he did, the young man would give Tim pointers and tips on how to improve his training. After a few days of this, Tim and the young man began scheduling their workouts together, meeting up at the gym for about an hour every evening after Tim shut down his restaurant. Tim also begins introducing him to his friends at the gym in an effort to help the young man gain clients. A few of his friends hire him, and the young man is very grateful to Tim for helping him out. The two quickly become friends. And despite their near twenty-year age difference, it's obvious Tim has taken to the young man and starting to become very fond of having him around.

One day after a workout, Tim invites him back to his place for dinner and drinks. There, the young man explains to Tim that he recently moved into town, and he doesn't yet have a place to stay. He shocks the hell out of Tim when he reveals that he's currently sleeping in his car, and using the gym to shower and was up, until he saves enough money to get a place of his own. Tim, feeling sorry for him, tells him that he can crash with him until he can get on his feet. Tim gives the young man the guest room, but from that very first night after dinner, the young man never sleeps in it. He sleeps with Tim in Tim's bed. Tim informs his boyfriend all about his young gym buddy he's decided to help out, holding back the fact that he's also having sex with him.

Soon, Tim and his houseguest begin to be seen a lot around town with each other. As they do, the more it appears that the two of them are much more than just friends, Tim really takes the young man under his wing. Being known as a very sharp dresser himself, Tim begins taking the young man shopping, re-doing his entire wardrobe. Where before meeting Tim the young man would only be seen in gym attire, or the same pair of jeans and a tee-shirt, Tim begins buying him expensive designer clothes and shoes. Tim also makes sure that he always has money in his pockets. The more time the two spend together, the more Tim falls for the young man, and the more dependent on Tim the young man becomes.

As expected, Tim's friends and loved ones begin to become very suspicious about the new guy that he is now taking care of. Among those who knew Tim well, it was believed that the young man is likely taking advantage of Tim's kind heartedness. But whenever any of them expressed their concerns with Tim, he would grow angry and tell everyone to mind their own business. So that's exactly what they all did. That is everyone except Tim's boyfriend eventually realized it was much more between Tim and his houseguest, and broke off their long-term relationship. But by that point, Tim's feelings were so strong for the young man, he didn't blink an eye when his boyfriend called things off. Because now he could openly date the young man without any guilty feelings about doing so. Tim and his new friend become inseparable. Rarely, if not at all, would you ever see Tim without his young lover by his side.

But soon after they began to live as a couple, and the young man became more and more comfortable with his position in Tim's life, the differences between their two personalities began to reveal itself. Tim was a sophisticated and educated gentleman. His idea of a good time was attending the theatre, dining out at fine restaurants, or simply lounging around the house sipping wine with a few close friends. The young man on the other hand like to do what most young men like to do, he liked to party. He started hanging out almost every night with the wrong crowd, often times returning home in the wee hours of the morning, intoxicated and drenched in the smell of marijuana. He also started making demands of Tim for more spending money and expensive gifts. When he wouldn't get his way, he'd react like a spoiled child, yelling and screaming until Tim would give in, which Tim usually did. And if that wasn't enough for Tim to deal with, he began hearing rumors about his young friend being seen out on the town in the arms of other men.

Within just a few months, the young man's behavior grew worse and worse. He began to openly disrespect Tim in front of people, including Tim's close friends and loved ones. Many of them stopped coming around, they were disappointed and angry with Tim because he was allowing this guy to demean him that way. But the more they would complain to Tim about it, the more Tim would turn against them. It seemed that everyone recognized the young man wasn't a good person, everyone that is but Tim, and his friends just couldn't understand why.

Then really crazy stuff begins to happen. Someone broke into Tim's locker at the gym and stole his very expensive Rolex watch, with Tim and the young man being the only two who knew it was in there. Tim began to find purchases on his credit cards that he didn't make. His Mercedes is banged-up after the young man returns home drunk after a night of partying. That debacle cost Tim thousands of dollars in repairs. Things started coming up missing around the house more and more often; jewelry, cash, even a new pair of Jordans that Tim purchased for himself as a birthday gift. One weekend while Tim's away on business, the young man throws a party without Tim's permission that gets so out of hand, the police had to be called to the house. When Tim came home and confronted him about the party, Tim showed up the next day at his restaurant with a black eye. Tim told everyone that the injured eye was from playing tennis. Unfortunately, no one believed him. Everyone knew how he got it, and who gave it to him.

But sometimes it takes a black eye to allow you to see what's really happening to you. Because it was soon after that black eye, that Tim began to voice concerns with his close friends about holes that he was finding in the stories that the young man had been telling him. For example, Tim found out that the young man had never worked as a personal trainer a day in his life. His parents weren't dead the way he claimed, they were alive and living well somewhere in Cleveland. Tim also discovered that he wasn't at all new in town, he had been living with another older man who had kicked him out of his home just a week before meeting Tim. In fact, the car that the young man was driving actually belonged to that previous guy. Tim became aware of this and all the other lies when the owner of the car showed up at the gym to take his car back. The car's owner caused a big scene, doing his best to expose the young man's personal business to as many people at the gym who would listen, and this included Tim. That day when Tim and the young man arrived home, Tim confronted the young man and asked him to move out. I'm not sure about all that happened the day, I only know that the young man killed Tim, stabbing him to death with a steak knife from Tim's kitchen.

CHAPTER FIVE

How To Avoid Becoming A Victim

Sub One:

If You Think It Can't Happen, It Likely Will

It's usually the confident swimmer who thinks they could never drown in deep water, that ends up drowning in deep water.

"The Scary biker"

A 6'5, 300-pound, draped in prison tattoos, leather jacket wearing biker gang member strolls down the street with complete confidence that no one in his right mind would be crazy enough to mess with him. He moves about not looking out for any potential danger; he moves about with no fear of anyone ever trying to victimize him. But unfortunately for the biker, it's actually his confidence and bravado that can be the exact thing that can make him become a target. That confidence and bravado, as well as his menacing appearance, might just be the thing that makes him appealing to a social predator.

Not paying attention and not being concerned with what lurks around him makes him the perfect target for someone who is unafraid and very proficient at what they do. His confidence makes him blind to trouble, and there's nothing better than blind prey. The cocky biker will never see it coming, he won't know what hit him. Remember, even the mighty lion who is the king of the jungle must keep an eye open for the much smaller hyena. Just because you are confident in who you are, don't become blind to the danger that's waiting to pounce.

"Thinking it could never happen to you"

I have a friend, who most would believe could never fall victim to a Hobosexual. Unfortunately, Karen did, and in an awful way. We're talking about a highly educated professional woman with an annual income of over 300k, owns her own home as well as a couple of rental properties. She also happened to be a self-proclaimed relationship therapist, a "miss know-it-all" when it came to affairs of the heart. For me and our mutual friends, Karen was someone who was strong, confident, and very disciplined in her approach to living her life. In my opinion, it was her confidence, influenced by those very strong personality traits, which made her a bit of a risk taker. And it was being a bit of a risk taker that made her vulnerable to being taken, which she was, she was taken in an awful way.

A Hobosexual was able to take Karen on a ten-month ride before she was able to recognize him for what he was and catch on to the game he was playing. Unfortunately it was too late, she found herself heartbroken and out of thousands of dollars before he disappeared back into whatever hole he crawled out of. I may be the only person she confided in about this. Our other friends and even her family wasn't aware of what happened to her.

She had moved a conman into her home for almost a year. He used her for a place to sleep, stole money from her, as well as damaging her personal credit, all the while claiming to love her and wanting to build a life with her. The situation devastated her to say the least, she ended up selling her home because she no longer felt safe living there. Her life was turned completely upside down, and inside out.

She later told me that she believed it was her arrogance and over-confidence that she could never be taken by a social con artist that made it possible for a social con-artist to take her. It was also her deep desire for love and companionship, combined with her feeling of invincibility, which kept her from spotting the obvious signs that she was dealing with a lying manipulator. Karen felt like she was unbreakable, until a man came along and broke her. Her belief that she was so strong that there was no need to be prepared, was the reason she should have been prepared.

It's likely that the Hobosexual spotted Karen's self-confidence and likely surmised that she could easily be conned because of her belief that no one would ever try to con her. And to the skilled Hobosexual that he was, that over confidence made her an easy victim. For the skilled Hobosexual, it was like a bank robber coming across a bank that is located next door to a police station. The bank is so confident that no one would be brave enough to rob them, that they don't even keep their money in a safe, they keep their money in a broom closet. They truly believed their money was secure, simply because of the police precinct being so close by. And it may have been secure, until a bank robber comes along who's smart enough to know that a bank located next door to a police precinct will most likely be lapsing in security. And now you have a bank who is supremely confident that they can't be robbed, about to be robbed because of their supreme confidence.

As you're reading this, there's women everywhere asking themselves, "How did this happen to me?" And trust me, not all these women are lonely and suffering from low self-esteem. Not all these women are weak minded, or women who aren't very street savvy. Many of these women are no different from you, no different than me; and no different from any other person who is confident in their ability to recognize bullshit when it's headed their way. Believing that you don't have any weaknesses could be one of your biggest weaknesses. Thinking you're invulnerable can make you vulnerable.

You see, it's usually a person who doesn't think that they can be taken who usually is willing to risk being taken. It's usually a person who believes that they will never lose, a person who is open to taking a gamble. It's normally the driver who's confident in his driving skills that's gonna be killed while driving at a very high rate of speed. A person who fears high speeds is usually someone who refrains from driving fast. You notice how in the movies it's always the couple who's not afraid to have sex in the woods who gets killed by the ax murderer in the woods? It's when you live your life thinking it can't happen to you, that it usually happens to you.

"They're better than you"

They are going to be better at telling a lie, than you are at recognizing a lie when you hear one. A Hobosexual is gonna be better with his ability to finding your cash, than you are at hiding your cash. Although you may think you're good at sex, chances are you're not as good as he's likely to be. He's gonna be better at convincing you than you are at convincing him, better at getting you to comply to his desires, than you could ever be at getting him to comply to yours. You're just not going to be as good as he is going to be. Assume he's going to be better at the relationship game, than you ever could imagine being. Don't fall into the trap of thinking he's not, it could be your downfall.

When survival is a person's motivation behind that thing that they're doing, you can best believe they're going to be very skilled at that thing. And they better be, their livelihood is depending on it. Where you may be casually getting to know him, he's serious about getting to know you, even if his seriousness appears casual. He may be your current option for a few good orgasms, while you're his current meal ticket. There's a difference between someone working a job because they simply enjoy what they do, and someone working the same job to keep a roof over their head.

You're no match when going up against a Hobosexual. And for the rare occasion, and I do mean rare occasion you may be better at something than him, he'll never allow you to use it against him. Remember he's a conman, and a conman convinces his victims to believe what he wants them to believe, what he needs them to believe. And if he's not better at a particular thing than you are, he'll fake as if he is. And his ability to fake doing something is going to be better than your ability to actually do that something. Because unlike you, his livelihood is depending on it.

And trust me, if the Hobosexual does allow you to believe you're smarter and stronger at something than he is, he's doing it for a reason. There's a method to his madness. Whatever he is allowing you to believe you're winning at, you're actually losing at it. Nothing with him is what it appears to be. But the problem is that if you don't know you're dealing with a conman, you most likely will accept what's happening as reality. And if you are believing in your heart that you have the upper hand in the relationship, he's gonna allow you to believe that. He's gonna allow you to believe that because it must be benefiting him.

You're setting yourself up to lose if you go into a situation with one and you're thinking you are in control. They are better at attacking, than you are at defending. If you ever suspect that you're dealing with someone who may be a Hobosexual, you must at once stop and separate yourself from them. Once you discover that he has lied to you, you must assume everything he has told you is a lie. Always assume that you are at a disadvantage. It's why it's so important to do your best not to allow one into your life. If he gets you alone, he's the smarter and stronger person in the room.

If I had a dime for every time a woman told me that it could never happen to her, I'd have too many dimes to count. More often than not, the woman who claims with confidence that it could never happen to her, is usually the same woman claiming it with a Hobosexual standing by her side. He knows it, and I know it, but she doesn't know it. These are the same women who end up ashamed, embarrassed, and humiliated. The same ones who spend the rest of their lives trying to figure out what they did wrong, and how they were so easily fooled.

"Beware of the convenient sleepover"

The social conman is going to depend on your confidence in your belief, that a sleepover is simply just a sleepover. Don't fall for it. Because for a Hobosexual, nothing is ever just that simple, especially a sleepover. What's a simple sleepover to you, is a way of introducing you to the idea of him living in your home. It's his way of trying to show you just how much fun and convenient him being there all the time can be. It's his way of getting you comfortable with it. The sleepover is to plant that live-in boyfriend seed into your brain, then everything that he does after that is meant to help that planted seed to sprout and blossom.

The convenient sleepover is like getting a sample serving of ice-cream that you've never tasted. If it's good, you're likely going to want a full serving of it. And that's what he's counting on, you badly wanting a full serving of him instead of that overnight sample. It's the trailer to his big film. The Hobosexual is allowing you to stick your toe in the pool in his attempt to get you to dive in.

He's not actually interested in having sex in your bed, he's interested in sleeping in your bed. He wants the ability to wake-up in your bed, not to have an orgasm in it. It's so easy for a convenient sleepover to turn into a temporary live-in situation, it can happen in a blink of an eye. One day a man you've recently met is falling asleep in your bed after a night of great sex, and before you know it, he's driving your kids to school every morning. The convenient sleepover allows you to see what it's like to experience having him as your man, instead of just your screwing partner.

Until you know a man very well, he should not be sleeping over in your home. There's no simpler way that I can put it. When you allow a man to sleep over in your home, you are likely sending messages that you may not be meaning to send. You are telling him that you are open to sharing your home. A man will assume you trust him, that you've moved past the getting to know him stage and now you've entered the wanting him to be your man stage. Regardless of if that's not the signal that you're trying to send him, he will interpret that signal his own way and run with it.

There's a difference between inviting a man over to your home for sex, and someone sleeping over in your bed after sex. I've found with most people, sex in their home and the sleepover go hand in hand. When it absolutely should not. One has nothing to do with the other, and unless you know a person very well, the two should never be combined. One act is for pleasure, and the other is for rest. While having sex with a man in your bed gives off one signal, allowing him to sleepover in your bed gives off a hell of a lot more. One means simply I want to get pleasure from you, while the other means I trust you and my home is open to you. Don't mix the two. Just because you're looking at it one way, you must understand that someone looking to use you is likely looking at it in a completely different way. And it's the way he's looking at it that you need to be concerned about, the way you're looking at it is truly irrelevant. Danger doesn't come from the point of view of the gazelle, danger comes from the point of view of the lion. How the gazelle interprets the interaction with the lion is irrelevant. How the lion is interpreting the interaction decides if the gazelle is dinner, or a dinner companion.

Be wary of a man that you don't know well who asks if he can sleepover. It's okay to say no. Always remember, sex does not involve sleeping, regardless of how much he may try to convince you otherwise. I don't recommend bringing a new man home for sex anyway, but if you do, insist that he leaves afterward. If he says that he wants to have breakfast with you in the morning, tell him to go home and return in the morning for breakfast. If you want to wake up next to him just as much as he wants to wake up with you, do it at his place and in his bed. I've had women tell me that for their own safety, they prefer a new man sleep over at their place instead of staying at his. But are you truly safer in your home? If you give that question some real thought, you'll find that neither place is safe when you're spending the night with someone that you truly don't know.

Sub Two:

Just Don't Take His Word For It

Normally what comes out of someone else's mouth is what they want you to hear, not necessarily what you need to hear.

"Check him out"

On this day in 2022, the average cost to run a basic online background check on someone was about forty-bucks. That's about the cost for a full tank of gas for a small vehicle, or the cost of a cheap dinner for two. Forty-bucks was just about the cost those days of a cell phone payment. And forty dollars is nothing compared to what it could cost you if you allowed the wrong man to come stay in your home. The wrong man having access to your home and personal information can and likely will cost you a thousand times that. A genuine Hobosexual will have you shelling out that amount so often and freely, you won't even realize that you're doing it. Let the wrong one in, and you'll later wish you had spent the forty-bucks to check him out.

A good background check is probably the best way to weed out scam artists and other folks who may not have the best intentions for you. It's a way to confirm if much of what a new person tells you is actually true or not. It's the best way to ensure that you're dealing with a person is who he says he is. If he tells you he just moved into town from Alaska, this is the way to confirm that. He claims to be a NASA astronaut, here's your way of ensuring that to be true. He says he's divorced with no children he's responsible for, well if you want to ensure any of that to be true, the background check is your easiest way to go. A decent background check will reveal patterns in his past that may help in proving or disproving any claims about his life that he's made to you.

For years I coached girls' youth basketball. And at the start of each season, the administration for the league would conduct a basic background check on me. Each year the league would do this, no exceptions. There was no way they were going to allow me around those young kids without doing their due diligence every season to ensure I was still living as a trustworthy citizen. The background check included searches for any criminal activity, as well as confirming my place of residence and employment. They used the background check to ensure everything that I had told them about myself, was absolutely the truth and nothing but the truth. The youth league conducted this check to make sure those young girls were safe when they were in my hands.

Conducting a basic background investigation on someone that you just meet and planning to move into your home is in my opinion mandatory in this current climate. It's one of the smartest things a woman can do. Not conducting one can place you in a very vulnerable position. I'm not implying that there's no chance of a conman slipping through the cracks of a background check, but it will greatly increase the chance that you will see something early on that may save you a lot of pain later.

People have asked me if a background check is something you must do in secret. Do you or should you notify the person that you're conducting one on, that you're going to run one? My answer is always no, you're not obligated to inform them. But you also don't have to hide it from them either. It's not against the law to fully vet someone that you are about to start seeing. Just as it isn't against the law to do a background check on a potential nanny or babysitter. Just like it's not against the law to properly vet a children's basketball coach. Once you consider sharing your life and home with a man, you have an obligation to ensure that this is not someone who could be a danger to you or anyone in your household.

He should respect the fact that you care enough for you and yours that you find it necessary to do so. Why would he have a problem with you knowing all there is about him? If he does have a problem with it, what could he be hiding? You should definitely check him out before he has access to your personal belongings, or before he comes around your children and other loved ones. Take a good look into his background before you start spending money on him, or before he starts borrowing your car. Sure, he may feel it's a bit intrusive, but so what? He should respect and even admire your desire to protect yourself. And if he doesn't, you shouldn't move forward with him. It's as simple as that.

"Scrutinize everything"

Until you know him a lot better, nothing that he says can be taken as gospel. Absolutely nothing. If he tells you that it's raining outside, you go to the window and check. He tells you he wears a size eleven shoe, the next time he takes off his shoes, you verify his shoe size. You initially check and double check everything that he tells you about himself. Leave no stone unturned. I know I sound paranoid, but you'll thank me later. A man who you don't know and you're considering allowing into your personal space must be properly vetted. And this only can be accomplished by scrutinizing everything that he says and does.

The way most women go about trying to figure out if a man is trustworthy or not, is by initially trusting him and then waiting for him to prove himself untrustworthy. But when dealing with a potential conman, that's just not a good approach. By the time you find out he's a liar, he's about a thousand lies in. By the time you find out he's a thief, he's possibly robbed you of nearly everything you have of value. And if you're waiting around to find out if he's an actual Hobosexual, he's lived in your home so long that he's receiving mail there, and your kids are already calling him stepdad. Until you know him well, everything he says and does needs to be heavily scrutinized to the best of your ability. Don't believe he has what he says he has until you get the opportunity to see and place your hands on it. In the initial stages of dating, don't believe he's going to do something until that thing is done. He can't just tell you he is who he says he is, and you simply accept that as fact. If you do, you are setting yourself up to possibly be taken advantage of. Make him prove himself worthy of your trust, make him prove himself worthy of sleeping in your bed.

Before you allow a man to stay overnight in your home, it's imperative that you not just take that man's word for anything. Make him prove and back-up everything that he tells you about himself And I mean everything from his name and birthplace, down to his place of employment, to his family and friends. If he claims his life is an open book, make him prove that claim. Ask him to let you read and verify everything that's written down inside that book. It's important that you know what and who you are dealing with, not what and who he represents to you as what and who you're dealing with.

"In the presence of his people"

Really no better way to check if what a man is telling you is the truth than by speaking to him in the presence of people who actually know him. People like his family and close friends. Those who know him well, who he would be extremely uncomfortable with lying or attempting to mislead you in front of. Unless a person is a true psychopath and very unbalanced, he will probably not intentionally lie about himself or about his past around folks who knows his truth. If someone would lie to you about themselves right in front of people that would know that they are lying, then it's safe to assume that he is capable of doing a hell of a lot worse when he has you alone.

If you have the luxury of getting to know someone while people are around that knows that person, take full advantage of it. Use that time to get to the bottom of things that you may be a bit confused about. Maybe there are things that he's told you about himself that you suspect may not be true. Or something that you believe to be true, but you would just like to have it confirmed. It's like the comfort that you get when going on a blind date, and the mutual friend who hooked you and your date up and also knows you both very well, is tagging along. It allows you to relax a bit more on the date. Alone with the person that you're trying to get to know, you have no one present that can co-sign what the date is telling you. But with the mutual friend who has a history with you both sitting at the table, your date will likely be reluctant to attempt to mislead you.

Ask questions, listen to his response, and watch how the friends react to his response. Is he overly nervous about having to answer your questions in front of his friends? Keep an eye open for any hesitation that he may have when talking in front of them. Watch to see if the tension in the room changes once you start asking him questions, or if he quickly tries to change the subject of conversation. Or if he just finds a reason to get the hell out of there. I find that most people who are trying to mislead you, if they have folks around that know them, will rather find a way to avoid the questions instead of trying to lie their way out.

Most women take the opposite approach in the beginning stages of getting to know a man. Women are usually reluctant to be around a new man's friends or family in an attempt to avoid their relationship being misconstrued as more serious than it actually is. But the fact is when you take this approach, you miss out on great opportunities to really get to know the guy that you're now seeing. It's nearly impossible to be someone you're not when you are around people who know who you are. Even for a seasoned conman, this would not make for a comfortable situation for him to be in.

"Remove your home from the equation"

The absolutely sure way to protect yourself from the efforts of a Hobosexual is to simply keep him out of your home, period! Take your home out of the equation when dealing with one and he is rendered powerless. Without access to where you rest your head, he cannot take advantage of you in order to rest his. Keeping a potential social predator out is the only way to keep home court advantage. He is in search of a place to sleep, sex from you is just a way to achieve this goal. It's your bedroom that he wants, it's your couch, it's your kitchen, and if he can't have access to it, he can't victimize you.

A Hobosexual who is denied access to your home will more than likely move on to find another sucker. He is looking for a roof over his head, he doesn't have time to waste on someone who is keeping the one thing away from him that he is looking for. You want to find out if a man is a Hobosexual, one sure way is to keep him out of your house and see how long he sticks around. Trust me, if he is a true conman, he won't be sticking around for long. He'll just disappear just as quick as he appeared. He is not looking for a new friend, or even a new lover, he needs someone who will essentially take care of him. He needs someone who is willing to open their home up to him, someone willing to share all that they have earned, so he doesn't have to put the work in earning anything for himself. If after you remove your home from the equation, he removes himself from the equation, you then will know exactly what you were dealing with.

You want to find out if someone is hanging out with you just because you spend money on them, stop spending money on them and watch how they react. Same thing with sex. You want to find out if someone is only dating you because of the wonderful time you give them in bed, stop rolling around in the sheets with them and see if they stick around. If it's your delicious cooking that you believe a new man is targeting, stay out of the kitchen and see what he does. Chances are most people are not gonna stick around if they can't get what they want out of you. Denying a Hobosexual access to your home is basically removing the one motivation that he has for interacting with you.

Sub Three:

Questions Needed To Be Asked & Answered

You need to get to the bottom of things.

"Why are you crashing on someone's couch?"

I think most women avoid asking certain questions of a man that they meet because they are trying to not come off as prying. They just don't ask certain questions because they fear scaring off the potential beau. They also don't want to appear as if their being judgmental. Some want to give the man an opportunity to be forthcoming with certain information about themselves when he becomes comfortable enough to do so. And believe it or not, many women that I've spoken to avoid asking certain questions because they really don't want to hear the answers. Unfortunately for these women, hell would freeze over before most men will offer up any information about themselves that could possibly jeopardize their chances of making it with you.

But there are questions that if not asked and properly answered in the very beginning, should make you very hesitant to continue getting to know a new person. Regardless of how cute and charismatic he is, there are some things you need to know before allowing him into your life, into your home, or into your bed. The first question we will tackle is in my opinion the most important, "Why are you sleeping on your friend's couch?" Followed up by, "How long have you been sleeping there?" Then hit him with, "Just what are you actively doing to rectify this situation?"

Some women will meet a man who doesn't have a pot-to-pee-in and won't ask any questions aimed at trying to find out why he doesn't own a pot. They'll just ignore it, even if they're bursting with curiosity. They may think they have found Mister Right, and they don't want to possibly rock the boat by coming off as a bit too nosey. Some women may even believe that it's just not any of their business on knowing why he's sleeping on a friend's sofa. When it most certainly is their business. You, a person with your own place, have an obligation to yourself to know why he doesn't have a place of his own. If he is crashing on a friend's couch, you need to become confident that he's not trying to get close to you so that he can have access to yours.

All of us has a story. Every position that you have ever found yourself in during your life, whether good or bad, there's a backstory that got you there. I joined the army and was stationed at Fort Hood, and that's how I ended up in Texas during the late 80's. Someone stole a car and that's how they ended up in jail. A person attended law school and that's how they ended up working as an attorney. Someone decided to sail around the world, and that's how they ended up being lost at sea. And a man who ends up on a friend's couch, also got there somehow. Something occurred in that man's life that resulted in him becoming homeless and crashing with a friend. And that story is a story that you need to hear.

You're not trying to judge the man for falling, you're just trying to get to the bottom of what caused the fall. You just want to make sure his current situation is not a circumstance due to some dubious or bad behavior on his part. You want to have these questions answered so that you can make sure you're dealing with an individual who's on the up-and-up. Asking questions and verifying the answers is the only way you can be sure that the person that is attempting to get close to you is someone that you can possibly trust. Finding out how a person ended up where they are when you meet them is particularly important if you're considering building a future with them.

"Why no job or income?"

Look, I've been unemployed before during various stages of my life. So, I'd be the first person to say that it happens to the best of us. Not having a job does not mean that you're a bad person. It doesn't automatically make you a Hobosexual. But it also should not excuse you from being ask the question, "Why are you not currently working, why don't you have a job?" It's a legitimate question to ask, especially from a woman who just met you and you're showing interest in dating. It's a question that a woman should require to be answered by any man she meets that does not have a source of income. Again, a man not working shouldn't necessarily make it a deal breaker. It just means more questions about the man must be asked, that's all.

You must be comfortable asking questions that may make the moment uncomfortable. No one wants to have to explain to someone that they've just met, why they are currently unemployed, or why they are in the financial state that they're in. But them becoming uncomfortable should not keep you from asking a question that you have a right to know the answer to. Any man gives you that right to ask that question the moment he expresses interest in you. A man who's trying to get to know you and doesn't agree that you have that right, that's a man you should avoid. You need to know if this unemployment situation is something that is recent and or rare for him, or if it's something that occurs a lot in his life.

You need to get an understanding of his attitude toward not being employed. Does he feel a since of urgency with finding a job? If he seems a bit too comfortable and relaxed with not working, this could be a sign of a much bigger issue. If he believes being unemployed should not interfere with the two of you entering into a relationship, it could be a sign that you have a potential Hobosexual on your hands.

Unless a man has made a personal choice to not be working, that man has no reason to feel ashamed or embarrassed. In life, things occur every day that can and will leave anyone jobless. We all know people who are unemployed and spend every waking moment searching for new employment. While at the same time we may know folks who are comfortable being out of work, and might even be leaching off those who care about them. It's your responsibility after meeting a new man to find out which of these two unemployed types he identifies with. Because if it's the latter, I recommend you proceed with caution. In fact, I recommend you don't proceed at all.

"Have you ever been locked-up?"

While doing my research, I was incredibly surprised to find that this is a question that most women said they never would ask a man when first getting to know him. It was really tough for me to believe. I actually couldn't find one woman that would ask this question. Some felt that there just wasn't a reason to, while others said that they just wouldn't have felt comfortable doing it. I believe it's one of the most important aspects of a man's past that a woman should be curious about. Has the guy that you just met and would like to begin dating have a criminal past that resulted in him ever being incarcerated? Outside of the "are you married or currently dating" question, what's more important than the "have you ever been convicted of a crime" question?

Many women don't find out that the man their seeing is an ex-con until they've had sex and often times have already started living with the man. Some even have brought men into the lives of their children only to find out later that the men had actually been convicted in the past of committing some type of child abuse. In many situations, some of these same men would end up abusing the children of these women. These stories shocked me. More time is spent scrutinizing men that are hired to stand post as a school crossing guard, than the men who women move into their home to live amongst their young children.

Very seldom are you gonna find a man interested in getting close to you, who is going to admit to having spent time in jail. Regardless of how honest he may be, it's just not information that he is going to offer without you inquiring about it. Most men aren't proud of their criminal past, so it may not only take you asking about it, but it may also take you insisting that he discuss it. It's one of those if you don't ask, how will you ever know situations. And it's definitely something that you need to know.

I really don't see what the reluctance is with asking a person that you meet if he's ever been locked-up. It seems like it would be an easy enough question to ask, just like any other question you would like the answer to. "Hey, do you prefer Coke or Pepsi?" "Do you have any children?" "Do you play poker?" "Can you swim?" "Do you like the taste of peas?" "Have you ever been locked-up?" It's damn sure more important to know if he's been to jail than if he watches horror movies. Would you rather know if a person takes cream in his coffee, or if he's ever robbed a bank? Would you rather know if he enjoys hiking, or if he has a record for writing bad checks, or stealing cars? I would hope it would be if he has a record for writing bad checks, since there's a good chance he's gonna soon have access to where you keep your check book. Shouldn't you want to know if he's ever stolen a car before you hand over the keys to yours?

Imagine if you let a new guy into your home and sometime later, he disappears with your tv. Then the police inform you that he has a long record of stealing tv's. Just how stupid and foolish do you think you would feel? And this foolishness happens all the time. You gotta know the background of someone that you're bringing into your home. Because if you don't, you could be placing you and yours in jeopardy. Remember, the only person who has the task and responsibility of protecting you, is you.

I don't want anyone to believe I'm bashing or trying to shame a person who may have been on the wrong side of the law sometime in their past. I'm simply suggesting that if they have, it's something that you should be aware of. I've been arrested once and convicted of misdemeanor assault. I don't consider myself a bad guy because of it. I made a mistake, hurt a guy during a fight, and later paid the cost for it. Luckily, I was given no jail time, and sentenced to one year probation, along with ninety days of anger management. Although I don't believe the conviction represents who I am or what I'm likely to do again, I do believe a woman that I'm attempting to get close to does have a right to ask me about it if she chooses to. It's a part of my history that I'm not proud of, just like aspects of my history that I am proud of.

"Why are you so comfortable dating while broke?"

You want to know why a man is so comfortable pursuing you when he has nothing to offer outside of sex. Why would he want something with you when he doesn't have anything to bring to the table? What level of respect for you does this man have that he thinks that pursuing you under these conditions would be acceptable? What does this say about the impression that you may have given him? Why is he so comfortable trying to date you when you have everything, and he has nothing? The fact is, in my opinion and it's just my opinion, no one should be comfortable dating if they can't even take care of themselves. To me, all of your time and energy should be focused on finding a job and a place to stay, if these are things that you don't have. I'd have to assume that he would only be comfortable dating you under these conditions because he's expecting you to facilitate the dating. The only reason your new man is not spending his every moment trying to get out of the ditch that he finds himself stuck in, is because he sees you as the way out of the ditch.

"Why are you comfortable pursuing me when you are under so much financial hardship?" It's hard for me to understand why women don't ask this question of men when they initially meet them. You should question his intentions, as well as his sense of responsibility and level of maturity. Most responsible men that you meet who may have fallen on tough times for whatever the reason, is not likely to want to be very social. He's more likely going to be too concerned and stressed-out with trying to repair his life, to be opening that life up to someone else. He most likely would not be at all comfortable attempting to date you unless he's looking for you to help resolve his current situation.

It says a lot about a man who does not feel at all ashamed or embarrassed, for a woman that he claims to like, to see him in the position of not being able to take care of himself. How a man you meet feels about you knowing he is struggling is very revealing about the man's state of mind. His self-respect must come into question. Instead of being overwhelmed by his good looks and charm, you need to also be focused on the man that he is. Finding yourself in a bad patch in life, absolutely does not mean that you're bad people. It's how you conduct yourself during that bad patch that should be judged by someone new that you meet.

The Story of Mr. Melton
"The Babysitting Stepdad"

When I'm writing, I spend a lot of time pecking away at my laptop in all types of coffee shops and internet lounges in whatever part of the country I may find myself in. I'm more productive when working in places like this instead of inside the quiet confines of my home. I've always found inspiration from being in the midst of life as it happens around me, it really gets my creative juices flowing. It's also a great way to meet people, as well as a good way to hear some wonderful and interesting real-life stories. On one memorable occasion when I was penning this project while hanging out in one of my favorite writing spots in Arlington, Virginia, a young man sitting nearby asked me what I was working on. This happens to me often, and I really don't mind it, I've actually gained some really wonderful friends this way. When I told him about this book, he pulled back a devilish grin and said, "Boy, do I have a story for you!"

Chris was just six years old when his parents divorced. He and his twin sister remained with their mom. Although their dad moved way across town, they spent nearly every weekend with him. That is until when Chris was around nine, his father remarried and started a new family of his own.

Then the visits with dad would slowly turn into once-a-month visits, then once every few months, until eventually he and his sister would see their father just a couple of weeks during each summer.

Chris's mom stayed single, never even really dating after the divorce. She spent most of her time working long hours at a nursing home, leaving Chris and his sister in the care of various family members and sitters. The only time Chris remembers really spending with his mother was at church, which the family attended faithfully a few times a week. Chris's mom was a deeply religious woman, and the church played a huge part in Chris and his sister's childhood. He, his mom, and his sister were very close. Despite not having a whole lot, Chris's mom made sure that the kids wanted for nothing, and that they always had fun when she was able to. Chris recalled all that changing the day of his eleventh birthday.

Chris best memory of this day was his mom coming home with a man he had never seen before. The stranger, who appeared to be someone who his mom was already very familiar with, was carrying a large box containing something Chris had been begging his mom to get him for over a year... a puppy. And for Chris, the puppy made it the best birthday of his young life. He received a number of gifts, but as hard as he could try when telling me this story, he couldn't remember anything else from that day but that small dog that he named Bugsy, and the face of the man who brought Bugsy home to him. But as happy as the day was, it also was a very weird day, because his mom never really explained who the mystery man was, she simply introduced him as Mr. Melton. It was also the day Mr. Melton moved in with them.

Chris's mom was a very private and conservative woman, someone who Chris never knew or had a reason to believe had any type of social life. Prior to Mr. Melton, the only man he ever even saw around his mother was when she was married to his father. At first, young Chris simply thought the strange man was the person who sold his mom the puppy. But it was soon very obvious even on that first day, that his mom and Mr. Melton was in fact very fond of each other, and that his mom was very taken by him. And just like that, with no discussion or reasons given, Chris and his sister now had a live-in stepdad.

Chris was excited about having a man in the house, even if it wasn't his actual father. In Chris's mind, after giving him Bugsy, Mr. Melton couldn't do any wrong. It was a bit slower going with his sister, Mr. Melton seemed to not be able to win her over regardless of how hard he tried. Chris believed she didn't initially take to him because he was just coming on to strong with trying to fit in. His sister had a close relationship with her dad, despite only really seeing him a couple weeks a year. Chris told me that he felt she probably thought Mr. Melton was trying to replace their father. Chris instead believed he just badly wanted to be a part of the family.

In the beginning, Chris's relationship with Mr. Melton was the type of relationship he always wanted to have with his own dad. Young Chris was really into sports, in particular football, and at that time he was playing on the neighborhood little league team. Mr. Melton would take him to every practice, as well as attend all his games on the weekends, something Chris's mom couldn't even do because of her long work hours. The two quickly became really close. It got to the point where if Chris needed help with anything, he would turn to Mr. Melton before taking the problem to his mother. He just felt since Mr. Melton was a guy like him, he tended to understand certain things better than his mother did. Like once when Chris got into trouble at school for fighting a kid who was teasing him, Chris was so happy that it was Mr. Melton who came and met with the teacher instead of his mom. His mom would have surely punished Chris, instead Chris and Mr. Melton just laughed about it as the two made their way home, and the school fight was never even mentioned again.

Everything seemed to be better for Chris after Mr. Melton came along. Even his curfew was pushed back a bit further. Before Mr. Melton, Chris couldn't play outside after school because his mom didn't get home until late. With Mr. Melton always there, he was able to play with his friends just outside the house until his bedtime. He would help Chris and his sister with their homework when they needed it, he even began attending school trips when their mother wasn't able to, which was most of the time. To Chris, Mr. Melton was a godsend.

Unfortunately for Mr. Melton, it seemed like as the weeks and months went by, the less Chris's sister cared for him. Though he tried to shower her with the same attention he gave Chris, it just didn't appear to be having an effect on her. In fact, the attention he showered her seemed to have the opposite effect that Mr. Melton wanted. But although it was as if she grew to like him less and less, that didn't stop Mr. Melton from doing more and more to try to win her over. If there was anything that his sister wanted, Mr. Melton made sure she got it. Any and everything he could do to put a smile on her face, he was very eager to give it a try. Chris recalled how finicky of an eater his sister was as a kid, so Mr. Melton made sure when he prepared meals, it would always be food that his sister liked to eat. Chris and his mom just couldn't understand why she just wasn't feeling Mr. Melton. And as far as Chris could remember, his sister never put into words why. She simply just didn't like him, no matter what he did for her.

After about a year of Mr. Melton living with them, Chris remembered how even though he was very young at the time, he began to think it was really odd that Mr. Melton was always home. He would be there in the morning when the kids woke-up, he would be there when the kids came home after school, and he would be there when they would go to bed at night. Neither their mom nor Mr. Melton ever talked about his job situation, it just wasn't a subject that ever came up. That is until one evening while the family was out having dinner at a restaurant, Chris's sister decided enough was enough and asked, "Mr. Melton, why you don't have a job?" And it was that day that the kids learned everything about Mr. Melton, as well as the story behind him and their mom.

Mr. Melton and their mom met at a church function, just a few weeks before Chris's eleventh birthday, and had been secretly seeing each other without the kids or anyone at the church knowing about it. Mr. Melton explained to the kids that when he met their mom, he had just moved in town after being medically discharged from the army because of a back injury that he suffered during the war in Iraq. It was actually because of his back injury that he was having a difficult time finding work that he could perform. But he promised the children that he was doing his best to find a job, and he was hopeful that he would have one very soon. That evening at dinner, Mr. Melton went on to tell him and his sister that he felt like God had brought him and their mom together. Chris remembered how happy it made his mother to hear him say that. She then told Mr. Melton that there was no rush on him finding a job, because she could handle all the bills until he did.

After dinner, Chris had a much better understanding of who Mr. Melton was and why his mom became so comfortable with him so quickly. She was a very spiritual person, and meeting Mr. Melton at church explained why she fell for him so fast. Looking back on it, his mom most likely looked at Mr. Melton as an answer to her prayers. Not only was he a man of God, but he also turned out to be a great man to have in the house to help raise her two children. And for the devoted mother that she was, that made Mr. Melton the man of her dreams.

So, Chris felt even better about Mr. Melton. Especially after learning he was also a war veteran wounded in battle, which in young Chris's eyes made him a superhero. Mr. Melton would spend hours some days just sitting around telling Chris tales from the war. Chris remembered like it was yesterday the story he had told him about how he was injured during his time in Iraq. It happened one night while his squad was out on patrol. The Humvee Mr. Melton and three members of his team was riding in came under heavy gunfire. In an attempt to find cover, they drove over a landmine, killing his friend who was driving and badly injuring the other two. The explosion blew Mr. Melton out of the Humvee, and he landed on his back in the middle of the road. Mr. Melton and the remaining members of his team was forced to hold off the enemy's attack all alone for close to an hour until help arrived. Again, to a young boy like Chris, that story made Mr. Melton bigger and badder than Superman.

Chris recalled it was that day at dinner that Mr. Melton informed him and his sister about his plan to marry their mom as soon as he gets on his feet. And after the marriage, he was going to move them out of the small house that they were living in at the time, and into a big home with a big yard for the kids to play in. He promised them that he was going to take them to amusement parks, on camping trips and vacations. It was all the things that a little boy like Chris and his young sister could want to hear from a new stepdad. But regardless of all the plans and grand promises, despite how excited it made Chris and his mother to hear them, Chris's sister was unimpressed and unmoved. Instead, she even appeared to be disappointed.

Time went on. It was the end of the school year and time for Chris and his sister to spend a couple weeks of the summer with their dad. Like every year, their dad showed up to pick them up and the kids were off. And just like every year, during the drive to their father's home, their dad had a ton of questions about what the kids had been up to since he last saw them. But most of all, he had a ton of questions about mom's new boyfriend Mr. Melton. Chris recalled he was the only one giving his dad answers, and how his sister who was usually very talkative during those summer rides with their father, was as quiet as a mouse. Their dad definitely noticed something just wasn't right with her. But regardless of how many times their father asked her, Chris's sister did not want to talk. Seeing that it was making her uncomfortable, their dad simply changed the subject.

It wasn't until about the third day of visiting their father, did their dad, now accompanied by his new wife, started asking questions again about Mr. Melton. This time when their dad noticed his daughter being reluctant to speak about him, their dad's wife took Chris's sister into another room to speak with her alone. After a few moments, his wife called his dad into the room with them. And what Chris told me happened that day after his dad joined them in that room, still made Chris visibly uncomfortable when telling me the story many, many years later.

After what seemed like a few seconds, Chris's father stormed out of that room, angrier than Chris had ever seen him before. His father's wife was trailing behind him, pleading with Chris's father to stop as he stormed toward the front door. But Chris's father was determined, and there was nothing that was going to stop him. Chris's father raced out of the house with his car keys in one hand, a black handgun in the other, and his wife close behind yelling for him to stop.

Chris peeped into the room where they left his sister, he could see her sitting on the edge of the bed crying. Chris then heard his dad's car speed out of the driveway. His stepmom returned back into the house and rejoined his sister in the room, closing the door behind her. Chris was left alone, completely confused about what was happening. And because he didn't actually witness it with his own eyes, what Chris told me happened next was the account of the story that his mom told him many years later.

Chris's father, pissed and armed with his handgun, drove back to Chris's mother's home that day. He kicked in the front door, shoved his way pass Chris's mom, and made his way into the bedroom where he found Mr. Melton. Without saying a word, he began to viciously pistol-whip Mr. Melton. He beat him so badly, that Mr. Melton had to be transported to the emergency room in near critical condition. Chris's dad was arrested on the spot, later charged with felony assault with a deadly weapon. At the hospital days later, after he regained consciousness, Mr. Melton was arrested and charged with multiple counts of child molestation against Chris's sister.

Needless to say, life changed for them all that day. Chris's sister had to spend some time in the hospital as well, and it was months before she was able to return to school. She would go on to receive therapy for quite a long time. Chris told me how after that day, it took him years to ever trust anyone ever again, especially anyone new who came around his family. He also never really lost the guilt that he felt for not protecting his sister the way he believed he should have. He pledged to himself to never let anything happen to her ever again.

Chris's dad eventually pleaded guilty to a lesser misdemeanor assault charge and wasn't given any jail time because it was his very first arrest. Chris believed the judge probably had taken into consideration what Mr. Melton had done when deciding his father's punishment. His dad blamed their mother for everything that happened. After putting his trial stuff behind him, Chris's father tried to get custody of Chris and his sister in an attempt to take them away from their mother. Although he wasn't successful in getting them, he did become much more of an active parent, much more of a presence in his kids' lives. Chris recalled how their father was around all the time after the situation with Mr. Melton. So much so, that for a while, it almost felt like their dad was living with them again.

Chris's mom suffered from so many mixed emotions after everything that happened. Anger, guilt, shock, shame, you name it, she felt it. She even for a brief time turned her back on her church for allowing someone like Mr. Melton to be a part of their congregation. She even expressed disappointment for Chris's father not shooting and killing Mr. Melton instead of beating him with the gun that day. And all those mixed emotions were amplified when days after everything happened, the detectives on the case came by the house, only to inform her of who they had discovered Mr. Melton really was. He was everything but what he actually claimed to be.

Turned out it was true that he was in the army, but he only served about a year of his four-year commitment. He never was in the war of desert storm, and he never injured his back. The real story of Mr. Melton's military career was that it was cut short after he was court martialed for inappropriate behavior with a fellow female soldier. He spent a year in the stockade, which is military prison, and then was dishonorably discharged. A few years after getting kicked out of the army, Mr. Melton was living in a homeless shelter until members of Chris's mom's church, who was doing volunteer work at the shelter, stepped in to help him get on his feet. Once the church took him in, Mr. Melton would go on to bounce around from one female church member's home to another, finally ending up with Chris's mom. The detectives informed them that during a stay with another woman at the church, the woman's fifteen-year-old niece accused Mr. Melton of touching her. But the girl's family for whatever reason not only refused to press charges, but they also refused to even inform the church about what happened. Mr. Melton escaped that situation, and simply moved on into another church member's home.

With all the women that the detectives were able to talk to, Mr. Melton's methods were always the same. He would move in, promise to build a life with the woman and her children if she had any, only to move on once the woman began to catch on to who and what he really was. Mr. Melton was a Hobosexual, and an extremely dangerous one at that. If Chris's sister did not tell their father's wife what was going on when she did, there's no telling what could have happened to her. A man who is willing to touch a child in that way is capable of doing almost anything. According to Chris, although Mr. Melton hadn't gotten around to actually having intercourse with her, there was no doubt in the detectives' minds that that's exactly what he was slowly grooming his sister for.

Unlike the previous family that Mr. Melton had victimized, Chris and his family was eager to press charges against him. He was eventually convicted and received life in prison for not only what he did to Chris's sister, but for three other crimes of misconduct with underage girls that he had been on the run for. Chris and his family moved on from the situation as best as they possibly could. At the time that I had the pleasure of getting to know Chris, I am happy to say that he and his sister were doing very well. Chris was working on his master's in psychology at a major university in Washington, DC. While his sister, who was married with a young daughter, was a family medicine physician in Memphis, Tennessee.

Out of all the folks that I spoke to for this project, this story hit me the hardest. Most likely because it involved a child being victimized, and I have a daughter of my own. It was also one of the stories that really motivated me to complete the book. Because if I were able to help keep just one young child like Chris's sister from falling prey to a predator like Mr. Melton, it would have made the years I spent pecking away at my keyboard, worth every peck.

CHAPTER SIX

What To Do If Victimized?

Once you find yourself under his thumb, there are specific steps you should take to escape from underneath it.

Sub One:

It's Confirmed, You Have A Hobosexual

Now that you know, here's what you do:

"Don't show your hand right away"

You now know for sure that the man staying with you is a conman. You know now that he's lying and misleading you, as well as having sex with you, just to maintain a place to live. You feel used and abused, you may even be heart broken. Then you become ashamed and embarrassed. And after that, you're pissed off. So much so, that you want to charge into the room where he is lounging on your couch, slap him upside the head with a frying pan, and kick him out onto the street. And you'd be justified in doing so, but it's not the most responsible way of solving your Hobosexual problem. Ridding yourself of a conman has to be done very carefully, for your own safety and future peace of mind. So instead, the very first thing you do after finding out what you're dealing with, is keep your mouth shut!

Don't let him know what you now know right away. Don't reveal your hand until you can properly prepare to smoothly transition him out of your home. The primary reason to do this is so that the moment that he finds out you know he is a fraud, is at a time when you are the safest, and hopefully it's at a time when he is at the at moment out of your house. You do this to minimize conversation, you do this to minimize the chance of him trying to give you trouble. You reveal what you know when you're equipped to handle anything that may occur during the eviction process. You want to do it when you are ready, when you're prepared, and he's most vulnerable.

Remember, you really don't know this dude. It may not be the safest thing to do to reveal what you now know about him when the two of you are alone, because you don't know how he will react or respond. Let him think everything is okay until you can get a support system in place, or until you can figure out the best day and time to confront him. It also gives you time to cross all your legal T's and dot all your legal I's. You want to be prepared, but you don't want him to be. Because his preparation may not be in your best interest. Like if he is also thief, by confronting him early, it may motivate him to steal. If he's possibly abusive, it gives him a chance to become abusive. So, keep your mouth shut, and secretly start getting prepared.

"Run him by the cops"

I know you're thinking since you're already aware that he's a conman, checking him out now seems unnecessary, but I assure you it's not. You already know that he's been deceiving you about his intentions, now you must try to find out what else has he been deceiving you about? Who is he really, what has he been involved in before involving himself with you? Has he actually been using your home as a place to live, or a place to hide-out? If you think this sounds farfetched, you would be greatly mistaken.

Take all the information that you know about him to your local authorities and have a criminal history check done. There are other ways to look at his personal life, like on background checking websites, but when it comes to a criminal history check, I always recommend allowing the police to do it for you. Because if it turns out that the person is a wanted fugitive, or isn't who he's claiming to be, they'll help you with confronting him and removing him from your home. If he is a problem, going to the police instantly makes them aware of the problem. And if he is actually wanted, who better to consult with than the cops? You won't have to try to figure out how you're going to get rid of him, they'll do it for you. If he is a fugitive, you don't want to confront him alone anyway. You want the law to handle it. Finding out a man has been misleading you in order to keep a roof over his head, is a hell of a lot different than finding out that it's a wanted criminal who has been misleading you to keep a roof over his head.

Let the cops check him out. Tell them that you have someone that is living with you who you suspect is not who he says he is. Tell them that you've discovered a lot of things that he's claimed about his past to not be true. That's usually enough for the police to at least run his name and or his aliases through the system to see what comes back. Fill them in on everything that he's told you. Anything that you can tell the cops helps them with figuring out who and what he may be.

Knowledge is power. The more you know, the better off you are in a situation where you find yourself having to confront someone who you don't really know. So, get the damn criminal history check done, it's for your own safety. You want to find out before making a person a possible enemy, if that person can be possibly dangerous. It's good to know if he has a known history of being violent before you have any type of face-off. If there's a history of reacting violently that you don't know about, then you risk becoming an addition to his history of violence.

"Get folks involved"

Make people aware of what's going on, what you're dealing with, and the danger that you possibly may be in. Because once you become aware that you're being victimized by a conman, that's the way you must look at it, as if you're possibly in danger. It's important that you make loved ones aware of what's going on. You need to have folks on stand-by and able to move at a moment's notice. You should have people keeping a close eye on you, your movements, and as well as an eye on the individual that you now know is taking advantage of you.

You must not only make your people aware of what's going on, but you must also make them aware of how you're handling the situation, how you're gonna go about resolving it. Your loved ones being aware of and accepting your thought-out plan is your best way of ensuring that removing the Hobosexual goes smoothly. You also must control your loved one's reaction. You don't want them to jump the gun and make the already tense and uncomfortable situation worse. It's very easy for an impulsive friend who cares about you to lose their patience and try to deal with the conman themselves, but you cannot allow that to happen. Again, your friends must stick to whatever plan you come up with.

When the time comes to confront him, if you can help it, don't look to do it alone. Plan to have someone on the scene that will have your back in case things don't go as you hope they do. The person you're confronting may also be reluctant to act foolishly if he sees you're not alone. He'll be a bit hesitant to try to explain himself or try to keep his con game going. But mainly, not being alone when you do it is for your own safety. You just never know how a person is going to react when you're about to make them homeless again. It's best that you have someone there with you when you pull that rug that he's been depending on from underneath his feet.

And use care when choosing the person or persons that's gonna be by your side when the time comes. Although a very masculine male would be the ideal person to have with you, the fact is it isn't really necessary. There's always the risk if you choose a friend who is too aggressive and confrontational, that the meeting could quickly turn into an assault on the Hobosexual, and both you and your friend could end up paying a heavy legal cost. You don't want to have a hot head with you unless you can definitely control that hot head. Everyone knows that an aggressive Pitbull is only under control until he's not. And when he's not, it's usually too late, and the situation is going to turn very ugly.

You don't necessarily need a bodyguard; you just want someone with you to show that you're not alone. You also want someone there to witness and cosign your demands. It not only lets the conman know that you mean what you're saying, it also lets him know that you are very serious about what you're saying. Telling someone when you're alone with them that you never want to see or talk to them ever again, has a different meaning and impact when you're saying it with other folks around.

Be careful not to have too many friends joining in on the confrontation and eviction. Sometimes a group can easily come off as a gang or mob. A small group of normally passive friends can quickly become rowdy if they believe someone that they care about is being mistreated. They most likely will already be a bit angry knowing that this person has been victimizing you, so a simple hello from the Hobosexual may be just enough to set one of them off. And a pack of wolves doesn't ask questions when one wolf makes a move, the rest of the pack will usually follow without hesitation.

The goal is to show him that you're not alone, not that he's being ganged up on. It may switch him from feeling like the victimizer, to feeling like the victim, and he may turn aggressive if he feels threatened. You want to get him to leave and never come back, not to get into a physical confrontation. So, make sure you have people there who understand the mission at hand, people on the same sheet of music as you.

One good strategy to use when confronting a conman living with you is to have someone by your side that the conman has never seen or met before, a person who is a complete stranger to him. It adds a bit of mystery to the situation for the person that you're evicting, because he won't have a clue who this person is. It could be a police officer for all he knows, a Kung Fu expert, a secret agent with a license to kill, you could have invited an armed security guard to back you up. Trust me when I tell you, having a person that is unknown to the Hobosexual can keep him calm and very cooperative. And calm and cooperative is how you want him to be.

"Time to get rid of him"

Now you know for sure what type of person you're dealing with. You know, but he doesn't know that you know. You've made your loved ones aware of your situation. You've decided when the confrontation is gonna go down, and who's gonna be there to support you when it does go down. You're ready to get him the hell out of your life for good. Only question now is, how do you go about doing it? It's not like a situation of a boyfriend living with you that you've grown out of love with, and you now want him gone. It's not like trying to divorce your husband. It's not like ending a roommate situation. You are about to throw a conman out of your home who has been using and possibly abusing you. You want them gone, never to contact you again, and you have no concern about where or how they end up. Still, you must manage this eviction with tact and precision.

It's very important that the confrontation takes place during the day, not at night. There are a number of reasons that you do this, first and foremost, it's for your own safety. But you also want to do it during the day because you don't want him to have any excuses on why he can't leave. Excuses like it's too late for him to find a place to go, it's too late for him to find transportation, or it's too late for him to get a friend to help him out.

Confronting him during the day makes it very difficult for the conman to come up with a reasonable excuse why he can't.

If you can, begin the eviction when the Hobosexual is not there. Use the time he's out of the house to gather the person or persons who's gonna stand by your side. You should have already discussed the plans with those friends, they should know the role that they're playing. And remember your friends are there for support, I would limit their involvement as much as possible. Next, collect all of his property and have it waiting for him by the door. Ensure that you don't damage anything because you don't want to give him any reason to cry victim as he's making his exit. Try to have his stuff bagged up and ready for him to haul away, not scattered about so that it takes him a bit of time to gather and pack everything himself. Once you tell him it's time to go, you want him to be able to leave as easy and as quickly as possible.

When he arrives and sees his property placed at the door, and you and your people waiting for him, he's gonna instantly know the gig is up. He may be nervous, possibly a bit defensive, so it's important that your conversation is short and to the point. You have no obligation to explain why you want him to leave and never contact you again, and I don't recommend you do so. He won't admit it but he's gonna know why you're doing what you're doing. So, there's no need to go into all of that. There's no need to reveal what you've found out about him, and how you found it all out. Him not knowing what you know and how you know keeps you at an advantage. The key to keeping the eviction going smoothly is keeping the conversation short and as one-sided as possible. As hard as it may be for you to do, don't show anger or aggression. Keep everything as cordial and impersonal as you possibly can. Say something like this:

"Dave, I need you to take your stuff and leave my home right away. And please do not return or attempt to contact me. If you do, I will be notifying the police."

Straight to the point. All he needs to know is that he is no longer welcome in your home. If he has a spare key, you ask for it as he is collecting his property. If he refuses to give it to you, that's when you place the first phone call to the authorities.

Chances are he's gonna attempt to explain himself. And if you begin revealing what you've discovered about him, it opens the door for him to try to refute those things, and you don't want that. You just want him gone. Have your phone at the ready to call the police and allow him to see that you do. If or when he tries to have a conversation, simply ignore him, and keep repeating that you just want him to leave. Again, if this doesn't work, call 9-1-1, and report him for trespassing.

Don't allow him to go any further into your home beyond where you have his things collected. No, he can't use the bathroom, no he can't have a glass of water, he must take his things and leave. If he believes he still has belongings in your home that you missed, ask him where the items are located, and you go get them for him. If for some reason you cannot find his property, tell him to leave an address where you can have it sent in the case that you come across his property later. But under no circumstances do you allow him to search your home himself for his missing property.

In the case of the Hobosexual already being in your home when you decide to confront him, your approach has to be a bit different. You still want to do it during the day. Go about your day as you normally would until your support team arrives. Once your back-up is there, you tell the Hobosexual exactly what he needs to hear:

"Dave, I need you to collect your stuff and leave my home right away. And please do not return or attempt to contact me. If you do, I will be notifying the police."

Because he's already in your house when you decide to confront him, you didn't have an opportunity to collect his property yourself. So, under supervision of you and your support team, give him a brief time to gather his belongings. Keep a close eye on him, you want to make sure that the only property he collects is his own. Once he's gathered everything, it's time for him to leave. No more conversation, no need for discussion. If he hesitates or tries to reason with you, you know what to do, start dialing.

What do you do if the Hobosexual claims he has no other place to go? This is a problem that many women find themselves dealing with. Most of these men really are going to be homeless when you put them out. Or even if they do have somewhere to go, they may not have a way to get there. So, what should you do? Well, each Hobosexual situation is different, you're going to have to use your best judgement when facing either scenario and only do what you feel comfortable doing.

Dealing with the scenario in which he has no place to go is really easy if you were to ask me; you kick him out regardless. I know this sounds a bit cruel, but once you discover someone is a conman and or thief, you can't allow that person to remain in your home under any circumstance. So, whether he is going to go sleep on someone else's couch, or if he's going to end up in a homeless shelter, this is something that you cannot concern yourself with. Approaching the problem of him having a place to go but no way of getting there can be a bit trickier. I always recommend if you can, pay for him a cab or a car service like an uber to get him where he needs to go. A good reason to take this route is so that you may know where he is in case you and or the police want to find him. Or if you were to find some property that he left behind, you'll know where to have it delivered.

If during your time with him you became friendly with any of his friends or family, contact them yourself and request that they come pick him up.

Don't be surprised that many of them, despite having love for the man, may not want to come to his rescue because they know what type of person he is, and they don't want that in their home neither. But although they may be reluctant, they may come get him if they know that he is about to be put out onto the street.

But regardless of how he gets out of there, or where he ends up, get out of there he must. So, remember the keys to successfully extracting a conman out of your home:

- Confront him during the day and try to have someone with you when you do.
- Collect his belongings yourself instead of allowing him to do it.
- Keep the conversation to a minimum, and do not allow him to move about your home without constant supervision.
- Ask him to leave and never contact you again. And if he refuses to do either, notify the police as soon as possible.
- Even if he does not have a place to go, under no circumstances can he stay.
- If he does have a place to go, but no way to get there, it's better to pay for a car service than to drive him yourself. But if you choose to drive him, take your support people along for the ride.

And keep in mind that your goal is to get him out without a hassle. So do your best, regardless of how angry you are, to stay as calm as you possibly can. Don't make matters any worse than they already are. How he leaves can have a lot to do with how he goes away, and how he stays away.

Sub Two:

He's Gone, Now What?

As soon as you get him out, here's what you gotta do next:

"Cut all ties"

Do everything within the law to ensure that the conman is out of your life completely, and for good. Cut any and all ties. You now know that he didn't mean you any good, therefore you must make sure that you stay as far from him as you can. The two of you should not have any communication of any kind. If he does reach out to you in any way, notify the cops at once. You have the right to file a police report against anyone that contacts you after you've asked them not to. And if they persist, they can be charged with harassment. If they return to your home after being told never to do so again, they can be charged with trespassing as well. And if he pops up at your job or somewhere that you're known to frequent, then they're subject to have stalking added to the charges.

If the Hobosexual has property that belongs to you and refuses to give it back, file a complaint right away. If he agrees to return your property, give him one chance and one chance only to do so. When it's time to get your stuff back, meet him in a public place, but not at your home. If you can, have a friend tag along. Remember he's a conman, so he may use this opportunity to try to explain himself, or he may even try to convince you to take him back. You are there only to retrieve your property, not for conversation.

Keep a record of any harassment. Once he is gone and has no reason to come near you ever again, you want to keep a detailed record of any attempts to contact you that he makes. This is especially important in case you ever have to file a complaint with the police. Keep a record of any phone calls, any visits he makes to your home or place of business. Make note of any contact that he makes with your family or friends, or if anyone tries to reach out to you on his behalf. He's out of your life and should have no cause to return under any circumstances. You must be clear with him that this is the way you want it to be, and if he ever contacts you again, you will consider it harassment.

"Change-up"

This man has lived inside your home, he's had access to aspects of your life that can make him extremely dangerous. He's a conman, perhaps even a thief, and it's safe to assume that he knows more about you than you think he knows. Understanding this, you're not only going to have to change all the security passwords and passcodes to your home, but in case he made copies of keys, you should have the locks on your doors changed as well. For your own safety, you must assume he's going to be a problem who has every intention of returning to do you harm.

Again, not all Hobosexuals will turn out to be dangerous. But unfortunately, it's one of those situations where you won't know until you know. And once you do finally know, it may be too late. You should know by now that you really didn't know the person that you had living with you, therefore you must move forward as if you're dealing with someone who may be looking to bring you harm. You must assume the worst about him, it's a good way of ensuring you stay proactive at keeping you and your home safe. Remember, a man is not a thief or burglar until he's caught stealing or burglarizing. He's not seen as a stalker until someone complains about him stalking. And a man is not considered a murderer until he murders.

Change your passwords and access codes to any alarm systems you have. Create new passcodes to your bank accounts, and if you feel the need to, replace your bank cards and credit cards. Even if you never gave him access to any of these things, you must accept the belief that he took it upon himself to gain the access, and you should respond accordingly. I've found credit card theft inside too many of the Hobosexual stories that I've come across. Assume he knows your account numbers, credit card numbers and even may have taken a couple of checks from your check book. You must go on the belief that he has enough information about your money to wipe you out clean. That's why you must do all that is necessary to ensure he doesn't get the chance to do so.

"The handy-dandy protective order"

A protective order is issued by the court to protect a person from being physically assaulted, threatened, stalked, or harassed. You may not feel you need one and in most cases the majority of victims don't, but I always recommend you get one anyway. It's really your call, only you can gauge how safe you believe you are with moving on with your life after he's gone. So, if you truly don't feel the need to get one, then don't. But at any time you feel threatened or in danger, apply for a protective order.

What I like about a protective order being used when dealing with a Hobosexual is that it not only makes law enforcement aware of your situation, but it at the same time informs the Hobosexual that law enforcement is aware of the situation. I also like the fact that he will be personally served the protective order documents by an officer of the court. The document is essentially a judge ordering him to stay away from you or he will be thrown in jail. And if that person is even considering harassing you in any way, the protective order most likely will make him think twice about doing it. On most cases it will make him too afraid to do it.

A protective order lets the person know that you are very serious about not being contacted. It adds a lot of weight to your words. Most social predators want to deal with you and you only, not anyone else, especially the cops. This is most certainly true if he has committed any crimes while living as a Hobosexual. A protective order can make him feel like he now has the justice system's eyes watching over him. How to file for one varies from state to state, so if you need one, I suggest you contact your local authorities for guidance.

"Don't stay alone for a bit"

For your own safety and peace of mind, after you've finally cleared your home of the person who was victimizing you, have a family member or a friend come stay with you for a few days. Now that you accept the fact that you really didn't know the person who you had living in your home, you should also accept the fact that you really don't know what he is capable of doing. You've exposed him for what he is, kicked him out, and may have made him homeless. An already disturbed person may not like the position that you put him in and may want to seek vengeance for it. You should not be alone until you're confident that he is out of your hair for good. You want someone with you for a few days so that if the Hobosexual does try to contact you, you want him to know that you're not at home alone.

If you can't find someone to come stay with you, if possible, go stay with a friend or loved one for a few days. First make sure your home is secure, and just get away for a while. Do your best to not let the conman have a clue about where you're going or when you're coming back. That way even if he goes against your wishes and tries to reach out to you, he can't. And if you do discover that he returned to your home while you were away, have him arrested for trespassing.

Staying with a friend gives you an opportunity to get away from all that has happened. A moment to re-group, a time to step back and take an assessment of everything. A time for you to clear your head, and to consider any necessary further steps that you can take to completely put the experience behind you. Often times if you remain in a home where you have gone through trauma, getting out of the home allows you to recover and heal a bit faster. Staying with a friend also is a good opportunity to discuss and reflect back on everything. And in doing so, hopefully it can help with turning your bad experience into a learning one.

Sub Three:

Your Show Must Go On

Just because a circus fires a clown, doesn't mean they close their show.

"Don't beat yourself up"

Remember you're a victim. It's not your fault that someone decided to bring this problem into your home. So don't beat yourself up, you didn't want to be a part of this foolishness. After finding out you've been taken advantage of in this way, it's quite natural to want to just crawl under a rock and never raise your head again. But please don't do that. These people do this for a living and their good at it. They lie, cheat, and mislead just to maintain a place to sleep. The idea is to learn from your experience, not to hide in shame from it.

Regardless of how you'll initially want to blame yourself for the man being able to scam you in this way, you are not at fault. Regardless of how smart, brilliant or even streetwise you believe you are, you're no match for a skilled and seasoned social predator. You're simply out of your league. You just can't beat yourself up for falling prey to this possible master craftsman. You were not the one who misrepresented herself to him, it was he who misrepresented himself to you, so coming down hard on yourself is not the fair thing to do. I reiterate, you're the victim, and not to be blamed for him choosing to do what he did to you, regardless of what missteps you may have taken when dealing with him.

Your situation is really no different than a person who accidently leaves her car door unlocked, and a thief steals the car. Yes, you must be more careful securing your vehicle, but it was not your fault that a criminal chose to steal it. You're not responsible for him choosing you to victimize. Your error in judgement does not justify him deciding to be a car thief. So as angry as you may feel, direct that anger toward the one who deserves the anger, the car thief.

It's the same way you can't beat yourself up for hiring an accountant who turns out to be crooked and steals money from you. Or the maid you trusted to clean your home who ended up robbing you blind. Would you be torturing yourself if you were to find out that the handyman you've put your trust in was over charging you for service he was performing in your home? Yes, be angry at the handyman for hustling you, but don't get down on yourself for it happening. Accept your responsibility for possibly hiring these people without checking their work history a bit more, but it's not your fault that they chose to be crooks and thieves. Your intentions were good, theirs were bad, and that's what you must focus on.

"Take responsibility for your mistakes"

One of the first steps at putting an experience with a Hobosexual behind you, is making an honest assessment of what role your choices may have played in what happened. You clearly were the victim, and you didn't ask the person to take advantage of you, but unfortunately your actions did help facilitate his ability to get close. If you don't take a close look at some things that you could have done differently, you'll be putting yourself in a position to possibly be victimized again in the future. And I'm sure you don't want that.

You asked the man to come in, but you didn't ask him to lie and mislead you. You're not responsible for him playing you dirty, but you do bear some responsibility for putting him in a position to play you that way. You should not feel down on yourself, because your intentions were good, but even good intentions can birth costly mistakes. Your job is to take an account of the things you possibly missed, or to identify things that you could have done differently. The sooner you're able to do that, the sooner you can move on with the understanding of what you may have done wrong and how to avoid committing those wrongs again.

It's easy to place all the responsibility of what happened in the hands of the Hobosexual, and for the most part, that's exactly where it belongs. But it is important for you to identify any mistakes you may have made and accept responsibility for them, so that you can avoid making those mistakes again. There's a difference between acknowledging mistakes and admitting guilt because of those mistakes. You're just taking responsibility for the choices that you may have made that resulted in you being vulnerable to attack. Look back on the entire experience and try to find things that you could have done differently. In attempting to put any bad experience behind you, one of the primary steps you must take is accepting the role that you may have played in causing that bad experience. You'll have an easier time forgiving yourself, if forgiving yourself is necessary for you.

"Revenge hurts the both of you"

Instead of being vengeful, celebrate in the fact that he is gone, you're no longer being victimized, and most importantly, you survived the experience. The truth is it could have ended up a hell of a lot worse than it did. Take stock of what you didn't lose, and in what you kept from the person that most likely was trying to take everything from you. There is nothing to gain by becoming a victimizer because some fool made you a victim. Don't lower yourself to his level by going after him for payback.

Instead of seeking revenge, direct that energy into becoming a better person in spite of the experience. Getting some payback will not ease your pain or end your suffering. It will not make things better, even if it gives you a brief feeling of satisfaction. Because it's going to be just that, a temporary feeling of satisfaction that you got back at the person that got you. Your focus should be directed toward healing, recovering, and keeping as far away from the Hobosexual as you possibly can. He put you in a hole, you want to dig yourself out, not make the hole deeper.

Nearly all the victims that I've spoken to, have told me how badly they wanted to seek vengeance on the men who victimized them. And unfortunately, some did. I heard everything from women having the man beat-up by family members, to one woman even assaulting the Hobosexual herself. Another told me how she smashed the windows and slashed the tires of the man's car. A few tried to expose and embarrass the guys by posting photos of them along with what they had done on social media sites. A woman I met in California told me how she had contacted the conman's mother and explained to her how her son was living. In almost every case, the satisfaction from trying to get some get-back was only temporary.

Victims have been forced to pay for damage to property after getting vengeance on men who have done them wrong. That definitely was the case where the woman took out her frustration on a man's car. I even heard a story of a Hobosexual who was able to get a protective order because a woman was harassing him after kicking him out of her home. He became the victim in the eyes of the law, all because the woman couldn't resist trying to make him pay for what he did to her. And if you think a greedy conman is above suing you to get money, you'd be greatly mistaken. Seeking vengeance will undoubtably make an already bad situation worse. So, seek recovery, not payback.

Instead of vengeance, try to get justice. I hope you understand the difference in the two. Justice is when you turn to the law to correct a wrong that has been done to you. While vengeance is you trying to personally punish someone in an attempt to get even. You seek vengeance because you want the Hobosexual to feel pain the way you felt pain. And the moment you do this, you switch from being the victim, to being a victimizer. He hurt you for his own personal gain, and now you are hurting him for your own personal gain. Although you are surely justified in wanting to do this, it's just not the healthiest approach to take. Cut your losses, regroup, and move on with your life, wiser and more responsible. Again, forget about vengeance, try to forget about him, and focus your energy on recovery.

"Share your story"

In no way am I trying to compare being the victim of a Hobosexual to being the victim of rape, but the reasons and reluctance behind both victims sometimes not wanting to share their stories are very, very similar. It's that feeling of shame, guilt, and embarrassment that force them to keep what happened to themselves. They often just refuse to talk about it, regardless of how devastated mentally, emotionally, and financially the experience has left them.

Most victims simply want to move on with their lives, trying their best to just put the experience behind them. Some truly feel that it'll just compound the pain to talk about it. And I'll be the first to say that a person victimized by either the rapist or the Hobosexual has the right to deal with the pain however they see fit. And no one should victimize them again by trying to force them to discuss what happened if they aren't ready to do so. But I must tell you, your reluctance and hesitation to share your story with others, is exactly the attitude that the conman is counting on you having. He's hoping you'll keep him and his behavior a secret.

Not talking about what happened to you is one of the reasons why a social predator such as a Hobosexual can continue to victimize women without the fear of being exposed and caught. Because the majority of the time, his victims, regardless of how bad of shape he leaves them in, are not going to share their stories with other potential victims. And in not doing so, it makes it very easy for him to jump from one bed to another, and another, and another. That's why it's just as important to tell your story, as it is to rid yourself of the man once you've discovered what he is.

With each person that you share your story with, you make it harder and harder for the conman to do what he did with you to someone else. Every time you share your story, he becomes less and less dangerous. Your silence can actually make life for the Hobosexual very easy, and I'm sure that's not something that you want to do. Make life difficult for those who are choosing to hurt people in this way. I don't believe you should be seeking vengeance, but trust me, telling any and everyone who will listen about your experience with the Hobosexual is definitely a way of getting some payback. You want to share your story, so that you lessen the chances of another innocent woman one day having to share a similar story.

The Story of Lou
"The Popular Couch Jumper"

The story I saved for last is one that I actually enjoy telling. It also happens to be the only Hobosexual encounter I get to discuss that doesn't end in heartbreak. It's a story that doesn't contain any mental and physical abuse, or money and property being stolen. In fact, it's not even a story where the people victimized felt like they were victimized, even though they were. The story of Lou is not your typical Hobosexual story, but a Hobosexual story it truly is.

One of the first things I did when I arrived in LA in the early nineties was find a fun and friendly place to play basketball. I hadn't been in town but a couple weeks before I came across the outdoor court at the YMCA on Santa Monica Boulevard in Hollywood. It had an indoor court as well, but because of the beautiful LA weather, back then, everyone seemed to prefer to play outside. And you could find open games there at any time, on any day of the week. It was there at this YMCA that I would spend a lot of my time playing ball and hanging out with some of the coolest guys I've ever known. A few of them, although we don't speak often, I still considered to be good friends when this project was written, over twenty-five years later. One of those cool dudes was my buddy, Lou.

Me, Lou, and three other guys at the YMCA became very, very close. They were already a tight group before I came along, but I was welcomed in with open arms, and I fit right in like a perfect screw. Soon after I linked up with them, when you saw one of us, you would usually find the rest of us somewhere close by. But although we were spending most of our free time together, which seemed like all the time, the five of us had separate and very different professional interests. One of the guys was well established in the modeling and fashion industry, another was making inroads in film animation, there was the aspiring actor, I was the comedy writer, and then there was Lou.

Lou was a bit different from the rest of us. At the time when we all were hanging out, I don't believe he was pursuing anything in showbusiness. As far as I could remember, the only thing I ever knew Lou to be interested in and even really good at, was hanging out and partying. He had been in Cali for just about two years before I met him and the guys. Lou was from the Midwest and had moved to LA soon after graduating from college. Not sure what he studied in school, but if I were to guess based off of the way he lived, I would have to say my buddy had a master's degree in nightlife. Because outside of playing ball, that's all I remember Lou ever taking part in. If he did have a passion for anything else, he surely didn't let us in on it.

Lou was also the only one amongst our group that didn't actually live in the Hollywood area in which the basketball court was located. When I first met Lou, he told me he had an apartment that he shared with his girlfriend somewhere out in Long Beach, just under an hour drive away from where I lived and from the YMCA. But I assumed that drive was no big deal for him, because Lou was on the court faithfully about noon every day of the week.

I remember like it was yesterday the first time I got to hang out with Lou and the guys outside of playing basketball. It was the second or third day of me being at the Y', and after we finished playing, Lou invited me to come out for drinks with him and the guys later that night. They were meeting up at a nightclub called Peanuts in Hollywood that just happened to be around the corner from the apartment where I was living at the time. Although it was close to me, I had never actually been inside the club. Peanuts was one of those exclusive night spots that at the time, was very popular with the celebrity crowd. I always wanted to check it out because whenever I would drive by, there would be a ton of gorgeous women lined-up outside. So when the guys invited me, I was super excited about going. Lou said he would add my name to the guestlist, and we all set a time to meet there later that evening.

When I arrived outside Peanuts, it was just like I expected, the place already had a big crowd outside, and there were sexy women everywhere. I remember thinking to myself, that I might as well turn around and go home, because there was no way I was getting inside this club. To tell you the truth, I would have been happy just mingling with the pretty girls who were outside trying to get in. But I wanted to hook up with Lou and the guys, plus I couldn't wait to see what it was like inside. So I slowly made my way through the crowd and up to the guy at the door who was checking names off of a clipboard. And sure enough, Lou came through, I was on the guest list. I'll never forget the "who the hell is this guy" look on all the folks faces who were in line as they watched the doorman guide me in.

Once inside, the first of the crew that I spotted was Lou, who was standing at the bar, mingling with a few really attractive women. I quickly made my way over, and I was taken aback by how he embraced and greeted me as if I were his best friend in the world. But it was Hollywood, everybody acted sort of fake like that, it was the way of the town. I usually stayed away from that type of foolishness, but those girls he had around him was fine as hell, so I went along for the ride and embraced Lou, my new best friend. And Lou didn't stop there, he then introduced me to the ladies like I was some bigtime Hollywood writer. Which of course at the time, was far from the truth. But I had to take my hat off to him, Lou knew exactly what he was doing. Because whatever he was telling them instantly made the women super, super friendly toward me. So, like I said, I went along for the ride.

Lou did this a lot with me that night, because he seemed to know everyone, and everyone seemed to know Lou. If he did cross paths with someone he didn't know, I watched as he would do his best to get to know them. We couldn't walk a few feet without someone stopping to chat with him, even a few celebrities that I recognized. It had me wondering if Lou was some sort of Hollywood big shot that I just didn't know about. I remember asking him if he was a club promotor because promotors were normally popular like that, but Lou simply laughed and shook his head no. Then finally, he and I met up with the rest of the guys from the Y', and boy did we have a blast that night. It was like I had known them all my life. We were young, single, and fully open to whatever fun that came our way.

The next day back on the basketball court, many of us including myself, were dragging a bit being a little hungover from all the drinking we had done the previous night. And the lack of sleep wasn't helping any of us either. But none of that mattered, we couldn't stop talking about the great time we had. In fact we had so much fun, Lou invited us to join him at a party at another club later that evening. And I didn't care how hungover I was, or how much sleep I hadn't gotten, there was no way I wasn't going to be there. Hell, I was already picking out my outfit in my head while we continued playing ball.

As we all were leaving the gym that day and I was making my way to my car, Lou catches up with me and asked me for a favor. He wanted to know if it would be okay if he went back to my apartment to shower and change clothes. You see he didn't want to drive all the way out to his place in Long Beach, only to have to turn around and come back to meet up with us at the club later. It made all the sense in the world to me, and I lived alone so

I didn't see a problem with him hanging out at my place until it was time to go out.

When Lou parked his car outside of my place and opened his trunk, I noticed it was filled with a few trash bags stuffed with clothes. I believe he had more clothes in his trunk than I did in my closet at the time. A big bag of clothes in the trunk just wasn't that abnormal because most people I knew in LA didn't have a washer and dryer in their apartment, they would just visit the laundromat a few times a month. So I assumed he was just really behind with his laundry. Lou grabs a change of clothes and his outfit for that night, and we make our way into my place. It was my first Los Angeles apartment, my tiny studio bachelor pad on Wilcox Avenue, just a block above the famous Hollywood Boulevard. I was still relatively new in town so all I had in it was my clothes, a bed, a sofa, a small table and chair that came with the apartment, my tv and PlayStation console. But anything that I did have, including any food in the fridge, Lou was more than welcomed to it. So we just hung out, eating hot dogs, and playing video games. He headed out to the party a couple of hours before I did because he wanted to be there to make sure anyone that he invited was able to get in without any problems. So he thanked me for allowing him to chill at my spot, and he left.

Hanging out with the guys that second night was very much like the first, it was a ton of fun. The Century Club in Century City was another very exclusive nightclub back in the 90's, and often times very difficult to get inside. But again, Lou had me and the guys on his own VIP guestlist, so we had no problem getting in. Because the place was so big inside, it took a little while before we all linked up with each other. Once we did, like in Peanuts the previous night, even if he didn't know them, everyone appeared in some way to know Lou.

To my surprise, Lou picked up where he left off the first night with what I then gathered he must just enjoy doing, he was again over exaggerating my credentials whenever introducing me to people, especially to women.

Although it initially made me uncomfortable, I must admit I really enjoyed the way it made the women super friendly, kissing and hugging on me before even telling me their names. With the ladies responding like that, he could have introduced me as the President of Walt Disney, and that's exactly who I would have pretended to be. You gotta keep in mind that this was way before the internet and social media, during those times it was very difficult to prove someone wasn't who they claimed to be in show business. The women seemed to really like and trust Lou, so if he told them I was a big time Hollywood writer, I was a big time Hollywood writer.

That night at the Century Club was also my first experience with what I call that weird side of the Hollywood party scene. Folks openly using all types of drugs, people having sex in the bathrooms, men and women getting damn near naked on the dance floor. The people were also so touchy feely. And I'm talking about touching parts of my body that only someone you've paid money for a good time could normally only get away with touching. I had random people bringing me drinks, some even offering me cocaine and other stuff that I didn't even know what it was. I was never into drugs so of course I didn't partake, and if I didn't watch the bartender make it, I wasn't drinking it. But amidst all that crazy stuff, me and the crew was having a blast, I really thought a night out couldn't get any better. That is until when everything was about to wrap-up and I was about to leave, Lou brought two very attractive women over and told me that they wanted to join us back at my place.

And just like that, Lou and I, along with two of the hottest chicks I'd ever seen but still to this day can't remember their names, are in my apartment around 3am for some late-night adult fun. The girls stayed for a few hours and left. Because we were planning to meet up at the basketball court later in the afternoon anyway, Lou asked if he could just crash on my couch until it was time to play ball. After the "after party" he just gave me, he could have asked for one of my kidneys, and I would have at least considered it.

He grabbed a change of clothes from his trunk and got some shuteye on the sofa.

Later that day at the YMCA, the Century Club shenanigans was all everyone wanted to talk about. Each guy in the crew who went had their own wild story to tell. I was no different. And of course, I had to brag about our extracurricular activities with the ladies we took back to my place. But to my surprise, none of the guys in the crew was impressed as I was with my afterparty story. Instead, they each began sharing their own stories of them and Lou involved in some adult fun with women after a night of partying. According to the guys, this was actually something Lou was known for. Putting it plainly, Lou had a knack for getting his friends laid.

We played ball for a couple of hours, but the night before took so much out of me that I was really a shell of myself on the court. Still, as tired as I was, I was hoping that Lou had another party that he was going to invite me to that night. But he never mentioned one. Buy I figured it probably was for the best, I was badly in need of a good night's sleep. After we finished the last game and everyone was heading to their cars, I noticed Lou leaving the court with Rick, another member of our small crew. I watched the guys have a brief conversation, then they both drove away, with Lou's car following behind Rick's. I figured they were just going to grab a burger at the Wendy's around the corner from the gym, something that we all would sometimes do together after playing. But then the next afternoon, I noticed that Lou and Rick arrived back at the Y' together, just like how they had left the previous day, with Lou's car following directly behind Rick's. As soon as they got on the court, Lou and Rick began boasting and bragging to us about all the fun that they had at a party the previous night.

I would be lying if I told you that I didn't feel a bit jealous as I listened to the two of them speaking about the good time that they had, especially since it sounded like an exact re-play of me and Lou's evening two nights earlier. According to Rick, after playing ball the day before, he and Lou went back to his place. There, they hung out until later that evening, Lou took Rick to a party at a nightclub. When the party was just about over, they hooked up with a couple of cute girls and took them back to Rick's apartment. You can guess what happened after that. And also according to Rick, that wasn't neither the first, nor the second time him and Lou had a night like that. Lou had not only done this with Rick more than once, but Lou had nights like this with all of the guys in the crew at least once or twice. It turned out that I was just the newest benefactor of Lou's popularity in the Los Angeles nightlife scene.

About a week had passed since that last night that I hung out with Lou. I had also taken a break from the basketball court for a couple of days just so I could catch up on some needed writing. Then one night around 2am, I get a knock on my door, it's Lou. He explained how he had been hanging out at a bar not too far from me, and he felt he may have had too much to drink, so he wanted to crash on my sofa to avoid risking driving home to Long Beach in his condition. He was my friend, and no way was I going to let him get back behind the wheel of his car. So I gave him a pillow and blanket, and we both got some sleep.

Later that morning, I had already been up for a few hours by the time Lou rose from the dead. Over some coffee and a light breakfast I threw together, Lou thanked me for letting him sleepover, then told me about the big industry event he was attending later that night. The BET Awards Show was being held that day, and he wanted to take me and the other guys to the official afterparty. He told me he really wanted me to go because there was going to be a lot of Hollywood big shots there, and it would be a great networking opportunity for me. I had never been to a real industry event, so I was really hyped about going. I had a few errands to run, so I wasn't planning on playing basketball that afternoon. But Lou was, and he asked me if he could come back to my apartment after he finished playing in order to get ready for the party. I didn't have a problem with him doing that, I even gave him a spare key in case I wasn't home when he finished up at the gym.

With the afterparty starting about nine, Lou and I were both showered, dressed and ready to leave around eight. Lou thought it would be a good idea if we rode together in my car and left his parked at my place. He said just in case he did some heavy drinking, or we got lucky and brought a couple of chicks home again. I liked the sound of that second part, so we jumped in my car and headed to the venue. The rest of the crew was meeting us outside the party, so that Lou could get us all in, because apparently this was a private event, and there was no way we were getting in without him.

The party was held at a very upscale club on Wilshire Boulevard in Beverly Hills, a ritzy part of town that up to that point, I had never ventured into before. Once inside, I gotta admit I was completely starstruck. Everywhere you looked there was some celebrity, a professional athlete, or music business bigshot. The other guys had been living in Los Angeles for a lot longer than me, so they were used to all the glitz and glamour. When we first walked in, I was so taken aback by what I was seeing, I accidently bumped into Wesley Snipes and nearly knocked his drank out of his hand. I remember it because I couldn't help thinking to myself how Wesley's films made him look so much bigger than he really was. I later of course came to understand that was the case with most action movie stars. As far as for the rest of the fellas I was with, it was just another party for them, no different than any other. It was definitely that way for Lou. Me and the guys got a big kick out of watching as he left us to go mingle, shaking hands and kissing cheeks as he disappeared into the crowd.

Two of the other guys spotted some people that they knew and walked off after them, leaving Rick and I alone at the bar. It wasn't soon after we were by ourselves that Rick told me that he noticed I had arrived at the party with Lou in my car. He asked if Lou had stayed with me the previous night, and I explained how he had gotten drunk at a bar the night before and didn't want to drive back home to Long Beach, so I just let him crash at my spot. I'll never forget the confused look that came across Rick's face, then he began laughing as if I had just told a joke, even though I wasn't aware I had told one.

Rick told me that Lou hadn't lived in Long Beach in quite a long time. In fact, he said Lou's ex-girlfriend in Long Beach had kicked Lou out of her apartment over a year ago. As far as Rick knew, Lou hadn't been back to Long Beach since. Rick knew this because Lou had stayed with him for an entire month after she put him out. And although he wasn't living with Rick now, Lou would sleep on Rick's sofa every now and then. Rick told me he didn't have a clue about where Lou was currently living. But one thing Rick knew for sure, it definitely wasn't Long Beach.

As Rick and I continued talking, another one of our friends in the crew approached. He too was surprised to hear what Rick was saying, especially since Lou had not only been telling that friend that he lived in Long Beach, but Lou also had been staying with that friend at least a couple times a week. And just like Rick and I, he also experienced Lou showing up at his door late at night, claiming to be drunk and needing a place to sleep. It turned out that it was his apartment that Lou had stayed in the night before he first crashed with me. Lou stayed with him after a night of partying, and then telling him that he didn't feel up to driving all the way home to Long Beach, just to turn around to come back to play basketball the next afternoon.

The discussion about Lou went on, even as the fourth member of the crew returned. Everyone had their own surprisingly very similar story to tell. Even after a few rounds of drinks, we were still swapping Lou adventures. Every now and then there would be a Lou spotting in the crowd of partygoers, but Lou was too busy being Lou to really hang out with us. And as great as I'm sure that party was that night, me and the other guys never would have noticed. We stood there in our own little world at the bar, laughing and joking about Lou until the lights came on signaling that it was time to go home.

Lou fell asleep the second he hit my passenger seat. During the entire ride back to my place, that talk I had with the other guys weighed heavily on my mind. Things about Lou that initially didn't make sense, now made sense to me. That night I got answers to a lot of questions that I had about him. Like why his trunk was full of basically everything he owned, down to his shoes? Why despite telling me he had a place in Long Beach, I never in the entire time of knowing him, ever heard of him going there? When we finally arrived back at my apartment that night, and I watched as he kicked off his shoes and fell asleep on my sofa, it all came together for me. Lou wasn't living in Long Beach, Lou was living with us.

I now understood why Lou would usually arrive to the gym with one guy from our crew, then later when we were finished playing, he would leave with another crew member. Lou would stay with one of us for a day or two, and before wearing out his welcome, he would move onto the couch of one of the others. And quite honestly, the other guys and I really didn't mind him sleeping over because we all liked him. He was never a problem for me, and I never once heard anyone complain about him. The only issue that I had, was that I didn't understand why he felt he couldn't be more honest with us about his situation. We all had become very tight, and I believe together, we could have figured out a way to get him back onto his feet. But unfortunately, for whatever reason he had, Lou never gave us that chance.

Lou was a Hobosexual, a Popular Couch Jumping Hobosexual to be specific. He was very likable, everyone loved having him around. And no one that I know of, including myself, ever had a problem with him sleeping over. He never left us feeling used, or like we were being taken advantage of. Although there's no denying the fact that he was lying to me and the guys, as well as omitting the truth about how he was really living, he just didn't leave any of us feeling like we were being misled or manipulated. We all agreed later that what we did for Lou, we would have done for any other member of the group.

When I told my friend Keisha the Lou story, she asked me how Lou could have been a Hobosexual when he wasn't having sex with his victims? Well, first we again must establish that Hobosexuality doesn't always involve sex. And in the case of Lou, it actually did, just not in the traditional way that we're accustomed to. No, Lou wasn't sleeping with us. But by taking us to parties and showing us a good time, as well as getting us laid by very attractive women, I believe Lou knew that it was highly likely that when he would ask to sleep over, we were not going to say no. I can't say for sure if that was Lou's motivation for hooking us up with girls, but looking back on it, it does come off that way. There's not much difference between a man sleeping with a woman to influence her to allow him to spend the night, and Lou getting us laid, or at least putting us in a situation where getting laid was a high probability, in order to influence us to allow him to spend the night. I believe it's also why Lou made it a habit of exaggerating our credentials when introducing me and the guys to women whenever we'd hangout. It wasn't necessarily for our benefit, but more for his. It was Hollywood, a place where people would do anything to be close to power, including sleeping with anyone that they thought had some. With Lou giving these women the impression that I was some writer who was a big deal in town, getting them to go home with me was a piece of cake.

This continued on with Lou for about a year. Every once and a while during that time, he would meet a woman with her own place and live with her for a month or so. Whenever he did, we would still hangout, he just wouldn't sleep over afterward. Me and the guys agreed that Lou must have had his reasons for keeping the truth about his situation from us, so we chose to respect that, and no one ever confronted him about it.

As the years rolled by, and life and careers took us all in different directions, me and the guys from the YMCA slowly begin to see less and less of each other. Eventually I got married and started a family, so my days of playing ball at the Y' and hanging out with the guys slowly came to an end. But those years I spent with them was some of the best times of my life. I've been able to stay connected with a few of them through social media, but rarely do I ever get to see any of them. When we do talk, we always bring up Lou and the great times that we had. I wish the guys all the best, and nothing but happiness and success.

The last time I saw or even spoke to Lou was at a small party that I gave at my place in LA in 2005. Then some years later, he popped up as a contestant on a very popular reality tv show, where I was happy to watch him win first place and the big cash prize. I was so proud of him. It always warms my heart whenever I hear about any of the guys from the Y' doing well, and that includes Lou. From my understanding, at the time of writing this, Lou was married with a couple of kids, and living well somewhere in California. His story is a perfect example of how someone can be a nice guy, a really good person, but fall on hard times and slip into the lifestyle of Hobosexuality.

EPILOGUE

Every resolution to a problematic issue originates within a conversation. The contents of these pages are meant to do just that, to initiate that conversation. The goal is to arm you with knowledge. The more knowledgeable you are about the lifestyle, the better equipped and proficient you'll be at protecting yourself from falling prey to it. If you don't truly understand a thing or why that thing does what it does, you could easily find yourself at the mercy of that thing. Again, it's a taboo topic. When I found it to be a subject of discussion that made most people uncomfortable, I knew it was a subject that wasn't being discussed enough, which was making most people vulnerable.

Whether you're a victim, a potential victim, or someone currently living as a Hobosexual, I hope you have gained an appreciation for the level of damage that this lifestyle can cause. The emotional, financial, and sometimes physical damage that a victim can be subjected to is obviously horrible. But for those who may be currently living or considering living as a Hobosexual, my goal was to make you aware that nothing positive comes out of it for you as well. As I hope that you now see, your life will be a day-to-day pressure cooker just waiting to blow, as conning your way through life will not give you that happy ending that you're searching for.

This book is meant to remove the Hobosexual's cloak of invisibility, that cloak powered by people's ignorance to his way of operating. It's my belief that it's the sheep that has no knowledge of the wolf's way of hunting, who is destined to become dinner. I want to make people comfortable with coming out about their experiences, regardless of the side of the situation that they fall on. I believe the more that we talk about it, the more people will come to understand that it does and can happen to any of us, even the best of us.

As long as it's consensual, I would never pass judgement on how two consenting adults choose to live with each other. If a woman knows that a man does not care for her and is only living there because he needs a place to stay, but she chooses to still take care of him, more power to her. I hope they live happily ever after. If a person is fully aware that the friend sleeping on their sofa has no intention on getting a job or paying a bill, and is still okay with that friend living there, I wish them both the best. But I can't condone the Hobosexual lifestyle because both parties are playing a game where one person is cheating, while the other player is playing honestly and within the rules.

Of course, when discussing this book, the obvious question that I always get is, have I ever lived as a Hobosexual? The answer is yes, a few times during the 90's after first arriving in LA, I briefly lived at various times with three different women who I was dating. In chapter one, I told you about my experience with Kimberly the hairstylist. It's something that I've never been proud of, and absolutely something that I regret doing. In fact, I don't think I've ever spoken about any of them prior to penning this project. There is no justification or excuse that I could give for doing it. The women really cared for me, and I took full advantage of it. I considered reaching out to them when I began this book in order to present to you their side of the experience, but I decided against it. Because truthfully, I don't even know if the women are aware that I did what I did to them. And in case they're not, I choose not to bring them any unnecessary pain now. But to anyone that was affected by my foolish and selfish behavior many years ago, please accept my deepest and most sincere apology.

Finally, let me say that it was not my intent to make you walk away from this experience hating Hobosexuals, but rather to help you understand and be able to recognize the lifestyle and those who may partake in it. The purpose of this project was three-fold: to enlighten, to entertain, and to initiate conversation. It's meant to be used as a flashlight to illuminate something that flourishes in the shadows. The book is meant to help create a comfortable space for victims to be able to share their experiences and concerns, and a space for potential victims to learn from those experiences. I also created this project in hopes that it can be a neutral and safe place where the sheep can learn from the wolf, and in turn, the wolf can learn from the sheep.

ACKNOWLEDGEMENTS

In no particular order, there's a bunch of people I would like to recognize and show my appreciation to for helping me complete this really wonderful journey:

Lute, who way back in the mid 90's, you not only inspired me to pick up a pen, but you taught me what to do with it. Thanks Bro'!

Grandma, Uncle Junior, Cousin Joanne, life became very precious to me after your deaths. And I became fanatical with not wasting time. I miss you, R.I.P.

Busboys and Poets of Arlington, thanks for making me feel at home all those days and nights I sat there pecking away at my laptop. It's me: extra hot vanilla Latte, whole milk, and a water no ice w/ straw. Best staff in the business.

Syd', quite simply the inspiration for all that I do. Your reaction to the book idea was priceless, "Gross, I'm not reading that dad!" Much love Buddha.

The many generous people who was gracious enough to share their stories with me, I thank and appreciate you all. Without you, this would have simply been a bunch of pages full of various opinions and speculations, instead of the true-life reading experience that you helped make it to be.

Walter L.H. the 2nd, my favorite YouTuber. It was your video years ago that planted the seed in my head. Keep up the good work.

And my family and friends who gave me all the space I needed to get done what I was so focused on getting done, thanks for your support and patience, because it's done!

ABOUT THE AUTHOR

A Maryland native, G.L. is also the author of The Switch Challenge: To change your life, you must change your life!" He splits his time as a writer in Los Angeles, and his home just outside of Washington, DC.

Made in the USA
Las Vegas, NV
26 April 2025

fc5fb3f6-bc4f-422d-86ff-be45f3ded089R01